The Pilg

Chrissy Smith

For Dad, always a good listener

Dear Reader

This story is based on fact and is a memoir and homage to those who lived and worked at the Pilgrims Rest.

Fictitious events have been intermingled with religious and historical truths and legends relating to the town of Saint Albans which have been passed down through the ages.

An ancient tunnel which links The Pilgrims Rest to St Albans Cathedral forms the basis of this mystical tale.

Chrissy Smith

PROLOGUE

Fiona Fordham reminisced for a moment or two before entering the old family residence at the top of Holywell Hill. As she stepped apprehensively through the same glass doorway the discordant chiming of the shop doorbell jarred as though it were ringing in the unwelcome changes which now lay before her.   Wistful images from another time were suddenly swept away, like the fragments of a fading dream, until nothing of any substance remained.

Swiftly covering her disappointment she turned to help her mother across the threshold and they both loitered for a while, moving around quietly on the soft carpeting, as they surveyed the interior of the new shop.

Fiona observed her Mother staring into the old, blackened fireplace, and realised thankfully that at least one original feature had been left undisturbed. She could see behind its wrought iron guard a flower arrangement strategically positioned to mask its murky centre.

Her mother's gaze was hard to fathom, was it sadness, or a silent longing for times gone by? So much had happened in this place and her countenance suggested she was far away, no doubt remembering the good times and the bad, the loved ones no longer here.

'Can I be of any assistance, ladies?'

A youngish man with brown shoulder length hair and laughing hazel eyes got up from his chair and moved towards them from the back of the shop. He had a pleasant, friendly manner and no doubt he thought they had come to enquire after the expensive, quality furnishings on display. Every corner of the various rooms in the shop was filled to capacity; rooms which once had been so familiar and dear to them both.

A familiar cacophony of sound suddenly invaded Fiona's thoughts and reverberated around the shop. No one else could hear it of course but to her it was almost tangible as she remembered the hustle and bustle of a crowd of customers queuing on this very spot long ago; but all of this was unknown to him of course.

'We used to live here some time ago' she enlightened him, 'many years back when it was a busy restaurant. It was called 'The Pilgrims Rest,' I don't suppose you've heard of it? It was run by our family from the mid fifties until the early eighties.'

His expression changed and he relaxed a little, shrugging off his marketing mantle.

'Ah I see,' he nodded and smiled, chuckling a little, as if the idea pleased him.

'Would you mind if we had a little look around?' Fiona asked.

'No, not at all, please feel free', he gestured with a flourish of his hand, presumably giving them permission to look wherever they wished.

He hovered near them for a while, seemingly glad of the distraction.

'This shop is only part of it you know' she offered, 'our family used to live upstairs, on the first and second floor as well.'

'Oh I see', he smiled at them both and then chatted on amiably, 'well not long after we moved in downstairs the upstairs area was taken on by a solicitor and an accountancy firm I believe. We only rent down here I'm afraid so I am not able to show you any other floors but if you'd like to knock on that black door over there,' he said pointing to a small alcove outside the shop window, 'through there you can gain access to the upper floors of the building. They were leased separately, you know, and turned into offices, but I am sure they wouldn't mind if you wanted to have a look around.   I understand a few alterations were made upstairs before we all moved in but as far as I know most of the original features were kept.'

Fiona quickly glanced at her mother who instantly shook her head and Fiona silently agreed. Did she really want to see what they'd done upstairs, spoiling yet more memories of how it used to be? Probably not, she decided; for the time being anyway, but perhaps another day, she might come back and take a look.

On the wall behind the young man, Fiona's eyes were drawn to a small glass picture frame which displayed an old and yellowed, slightly crumpled drawing.

'Excuse me, but what is that?' she asked.

He turned to follow her gaze, 'Ah yes, you would probably be very interested in this', he said, as they all moved closer. 'This drawing was found behind a plastered wall during the refurbishment and we've had it authenticated as a 16th century map of the original building.'

Fiona's heart began pounding as she bent forward, intrigued, eagerly feasting her eyes on the map, something she wished she'd seen a long time ago. If only she had more time to study it in detail, she mused.

The man lightly tapped his forehead as he suddenly remembered something,

'Of course, you've just reminded me, we found something else during some later building works, it was in the cellar, an old bible, with a note tucked inside it addressed to someone called Fiona,' the young man advised.

Fiona and her mother exchanged a look of astonishment.

'Well, how strange, I would imagine that is probably meant for me' she informed him, trying to remain nonchalant, 'I'm Fiona, Fiona Fordham!'

'Well goodness me, that really is great news,' he said sounding pleased and a little relieved. 'I'll go and get it for you at once', he declared as he turned and started to move away, 'of course the note was sealed so we didn't open it, we just popped it in the office drawer......... for safekeeping', he called out breathlessly as he dashed off to the back of the shop.

'That's strange darling isn't it' exclaimed Jean, Fiona's mother. 'I wonder who that could be from.'

'I haven't the foggiest' Fiona replied as she turned away from her mother's curiosity, feeling a fraud, because in her heart she already knew.

The young man returned speedily and handed her a small ornate bible, with a grubby looking envelope which poked out from between the pages.   She took it gratefully but his obvious optimism that she might read it in front of him was soon dashed as she popped it straight into her bag.

'Is the cellar still in use?' Fiona queried, looking at the familiar door behind him.

'No, not really, it's more or less empty at the moment, but we can go down there if you'd like' he offered, smiling encouragingly at them both.

Fiona cleverly disguised the rising turmoil inside her and returned his smile with feigned composure.

'Yes, please,' she replied as calmly as she could manage, 'I'm sorry if we are keeping you from your work.'

'Oh no don't worry about that at all, it's been so tediously quiet in here today, you are a welcome diversion!'

His amiable answer soothed away any misgivings they may have had and together they walked a few steps to the cellar door. He proceeded to lift the same heavy black latch she had used herself many times before and the slatted wooden door creaked open.

Fiona moved forward and peered down to the bottom of the wooden steps as a shiver of unease took hold. The young man went down first and Fiona followed, turning to help her mother negotiate the steep, circular staircase. As soon as they reached the cellar floor, Fiona remembered the strange smell emanating from this place, an earthy, damp odour with a hint of something sickly sweet.

As she looked around and across the room into the darkest corner of the cellar, she was surprised, but strangely comforted to know that, yes, it was still there.

The Pilgrims Rest

Chapter One:

The 'ladies' was a small panelled alcove in the luxuriously carpeted lobby behind Anna's room.   It was carefully screened from the diners' view by prettily patterned curtains and in the corner was a small Victorian sink and mirror. The 'gents' could be found after a longish walk across the courtyard garden, through the outbuildings housing the potato pile, and then on past the scullery.

Arthur Mullard, the comedian, had once poked his beaming face through the scullery sash window, and spoken to the girls who were washing up. 'What a lovely drop o' grub,' he'd said generously and Elsie and Jane hadn't stopped talking about it for weeks.

The kitchen was the hub of the place, a warm, welcoming hive of activity. During the busy lunchtime period it was 'all hands to the deck' and family members would remain stationed at their various posts; either plating up from the oven, replenishing the vegetable pots, dishing up the desserts, or arranging crisp fresh salads, each had their own area of responsibility. Precision timing was of the utmost importance so that all food was ready for that first customer to arrive and place their order.

Dougie Fordham, the third born of the four sons, was the vegetable chief and could often be seen surrounded by great clouds of suffocating steam as he poured large tubs of hand chipped potatoes into vast vats of hot oil. As the wet potatoes hit the heat a deafening roar would crescendo, becoming quite frightening in its intensity, as bubbles massed from within taking on a life form of their own.   Eventually after several moments the temperature would regulate itself inside the vat and the sound subside reassuringly to a slow simmering sizzle.

George and Winifred Fordham, 'Win' for short, were the owners of the restaurant and together they ran the Fordham family firm.

A formidable pair, the two of them took charge of the hulking great joints of meat which they always managed to cook to perfection in the large blackened heavy duty oven.

The oven itself was a magnificent industrial antique with five separate shelves, each shelf having its own thick metal door with large ornate handles.   These handles could be lifted slightly to release the catch enabling the door to be lowered and then lie flat so that anything inside could be manoeuvred forward easily for checking or basting.

During most mornings, when the restaurant area was quieter with just a few people in for coffee and cake, Jean and Susan, the daughters in law, would beaver away either side of the large kitchen table.   Their white heavy-duty cotton aprons covered in flour as they worked and kneaded their nimble fingers into the sweet and savoury pastry waiting to be transformed into the mouth-watering meat and fruit pies. And also, of course, the famous mince pies which every year caused a crazy customer 'stampede' during the run up to Christmas.

Out of the most basic ingredients, they would also create the famous 'Pilgrims Rest' rock cakes which were highly sought after for their delicately crisp outside and soft, fluffy centre. Within each rock cake was found plump round raisins, spread evenly throughout, and each melting mouthful was 'heaven' on the tongue.

Every day, mountains of mince pies, scones and rock cakes were piled on to plates ready to be displayed in the shop window and, once in place, the queue of people who had been patiently waiting outside would be let in. The cakes would be carefully counted for each customer; half a dozen or a dozen even, and then placed into white paper bags, either, small, medium or large. Once safely inside, the bag would be flipped over and the corners twisted to hold in the goodness.

A limit had been set, long before, on the number of cakes that could be bought at any one time to ensure there were ample supplies for everyone. In the early years there had been many disappointed customers who'd arrived at the front of the queue only to find that all the cakes had gone.

The Fordham family were extremely proud to advertise that all their meals were home cooked, their menu prices couldn't be beaten anywhere in the town and customer complaints were very rare, in fact regulars would return again and again, on a weekly or even a daily basis, to savour what was on offer. The reputation of The Pilgrims Rest was renowned ensuring it was full to bursting every single day with barely a table free in any of the dining rooms. Into this busy, hectic, daily routine Dougie and Jean's eldest child, Fiona, was born.

Once out of the pram, Fiona would often be relegated to sit on an old stool in the corner of the kitchen, tucked in the alcove between the cutlery trays and the shelves of crockery, where she would contentedly observe the comings and goings of waitresses and visitors alike, always remembering to keep well out of the way of the important business to hand... making money!

Anna, known fondly as the 'German waitress,' was an adoring semi-surrogate mother to Fiona and, about eighteen months later, her younger sister Caroline. Anna was married to Fred, a good humoured gentle man, often seen loitering around the drinks area while he waited for Anna to finish work. They had no children of their own, whether by design or just bad luck no one had ever ventured to ask, but both had served the family well for many years. Anna was a loyal employee and hard worker, enjoying generous tips from her regulars.

Her attire was more often than not a lightly patterned cotton dress, navy being her favoured colour, with a white lace collar and short sleeves. Her hair was light brown and brushed back off her face with a soft natural wave. She was formidable in her pursuit of tips and would allow nothing to stand in her way, particularly other waitresses and there was always noisy competition verging on battle whenever the plates of food were ready for delivery as to whose order it was!

She would amuse Fiona with her arrogant lunchtime antics by charging bullishly into the crowded kitchen, barking her food orders at Jean or Susan, or whoever happened to be plating up that day, penetrating the gentle din with her clipped German accent. Her customary American tan tights were baggy all the way down until they spurted out at the end of her size ten feet ensuring a constant flip flop noise as she walked. Her sprawling toes hanging over the front edge of her ill-fitting men's sandals completed the comic look.

The menu choice was always kept fairly minimal; Chicken, Pork, Beef, Lamb or Pie and on Fridays there would be fish and chips and of course in the middle of the week Grandad George's special of the day; a Chicken Fricassee perhaps or one of his special curries with ample measures of currants or sultanas thrown in, whatever he had to hand!

In the hot summer months, a cool crisp salad would be on offer; mouth wateringly good; using the freshest ingredients, sliced beetroot on top, a boiled egg halved and always two triangles of bread and butter on the side.

Jean normally typed the menus on an old black Smith Corona typewriter. The keys would noisily repeat clackety clack as the metal fingers drummed against the carbon ribbon and Fiona would watch in awe as her mother's fingers flew across the keys at such a speed completely entranced as words appeared on the page as if by magic. Most of the time her mother made no mistakes but if she ever did she would tear the paper out of the gripper in annoyance and once again carefully place carbons between each small sheet of white paper, feeding them around the drum, to start all over again.

When Jean had accomplished the task to her satisfaction she would whip the menus out, separating each paper copy from the carbon sheets and pass them to Fiona, whose job it was to carefully position these thin, flimsy sheets behind the clear plastic of the menu holders ready for the customers to contemplate.

The various rooms downstairs and the living quarters on the upper two levels were brimming with history. Built in the sixteenth century the building had slightly sloping floors, uneven walls and cracked ceilings. A red brick facade had been added to the frontage of the property during the Victorian era but underneath was the original timber construction of medieval times. It contained many passages, connecting rooms, and corridors, a spooky attic on the top floor and a dark, dingy cellar which could be found at the bottom of 13 wooden steps.

The cellar housed a vast number of cash and carry boxes of various shapes and sizes, all piled higgledy-piggledy on top of each other, containing all types of tinned food and packaged products, filling almost every square inch of floor space, with hardly any room to move between them.

One small bulb hung down from the middle of a low ceiling always draped in dusty cobwebs. It lit the cellar, dimly, casting long dark shadows towards the recess at the far corner and it was here that Fiona had first seen the tunnel.

She had been sent down to the cellar by her mother to fetch some paper napkins for Anna and also to help her fold them ready for the onslaught of the lunchtime customers. In the past Fiona had always made excuses not to go down to the cellar. She didn't really know why she should be anxious but she just didn't like the feeling of being alone down there, cut off from the rest of the house, the noise and laughter upstairs would become more subdued and distant making her feel a little vulnerable but on that particular day her mother was insistent.

'Go and help Anna' she scolded 'and stop being so silly.'

'Ok,' Fiona replied reluctantly, not feeling very brave.

She realised her mother thought she was just being lazy which wasn't true at all. She didn't mind helping Anna and always liked to feel involved and useful rather than being sent upstairs to look after her little brother Danny and two younger sisters, Caroline and Helen.

Realising on this occasion she had no choice Fiona sloped off towards the cellar.

On reaching the cellar door at the end of the passageway she lifted the latch and leaned forward to switch on the light. Peering downwards she held on to the rail for support negotiating the wooden spiral steps slowly and carefully one by one. At the bottom step she looked around searchingly amongst the myriad piles of boxes and tins spread haphazardly across the floor and crammed into every square inch available. Eventually she spied the crisp white serviettes; cellophane wrapped, and perched quite high and out of reach on top of a pile of boxes.

Catching sight of an old wooden wheel-back chair leaning against the wall she quickly grabbed it and pulled it into position so she could stand on it to reach one of the packets. As she teetered precariously on the chair she accidentally knocked the bulb which started to swing from side to side casting eerie shadows. She caught hold of it gingerly trying not to touch the matted grey cobwebs which adorned it lifting it aloft to see a little more clearly.

Her attention was drawn to the shadowy darkness at the back of the cellar almost sinister as it lurked in the corner in sharp contrast to the old whitewashed brick wall. Curiously, as she shone the bulb towards it, she noticed the bricks at the far end of the wall seemed to melt away and there appeared to be a long dark gap behind them.

There was no possible way she could get across the cellar to investigate because there were so many boxes and large heavy tins piled up in front of her. It was strange, she thought to herself, that on the few occasions she had visited the cellar before, she had never noticed it?

She shivered in the cold stillness, her heart beating loudly and matching the ticking tone of her wrist watch. She glanced down at the time and realised she needed to get a move on, the lunchtime customers would be arriving soon.

She quickly grabbed the packet of napkins and clambered down from the chair, scraping it back clumsily to its original position, before racing up the cellar stairs. She flicked off the light switch at the top immediately shrouding the cellar in darkness and quickly exited through the black wooden door pulling it firmly shut behind her.

She was constantly being lectured to make sure the cellar door was shut securely because of the steep drop behind it and so after making sure the latch was tight she turned the key in the lock before making her way back along the side passage.

As she entered the passageway she almost collided with Alf who was just coming around the corner.

Alf stopped abruptly and gave her a withering look as if to say 'you move' and so she awkwardly reversed into a small gap between the boxes to allow him to pass. She hugged the box of serviettes tightly to her and waited as he shuffled past. He didn't look at her again but did lightly touch the front of his flat cap in brief deference to her presence, muttering a gruff platitude under his breath.

Alf, a reclusive character who worked at the restaurant, lived upstairs in a small room on the top floor opposite the attic. His gloomy expression was a permanent fixture on his somewhat craggy face and there appeared something odd about him that Fiona couldn't quite fathom; he definitely seemed a bit shifty, almost as if he was up to something, but Fiona effortlessly shrugged off her suspicions and ran forwards once again through the passageway.

At the end of the passageway she did a quick U-turn to the right and rushed through the heavyweight curtains into Anna's room. Anna was sitting at the small table for two immediately to the left of the curtained doorway and tucked against the wall. She plonked herself down opposite Anna, and tore open the packet of napkins, her heart was still thumping from her earlier exertions and her breath came in short bursts.

'Well, there you are at last' Anna exclaimed looking up. 'I was beginning to give up hope. I thought you must have found something better to do with your time!'

Fiona smiled up at the familiar face of her old friend but she could sense Anna was not very pleased about the delay and was becoming agitated. Time was moving on and Anna was always anxious that everything should be ready before the first customers arrived.

She tutted and clucked like a mother hen as she sorted the pile of napkins, pushing half towards Fiona. 'Hurry now Fiona, we must be quick, we're a bit late today. What took you so long anyway?'

Fiona was curious about what she'd seen in the cellar and wondered if she should mention the tunnel to Anna. As she looked up at Anna's bowed head, she ventured a question;

'Anna, did you know that there is some sort of tunnel in the cellar?

Anna continued with her folding and did not look up. She was focused on the job in hand and would not be distracted. Fiona repeated her question and paused in her folding duties, finally earning her a taciturn response;

 'Tunnel, what tunnel?' Anna replied in an exasperated tone. 'Come on now quickly, do you remember how to do the folds?'

'Yes, I think so' answered Fiona, 'you fold it in the middle like this and then the corners fold in backwards like this. Well it's not difficult is it Anna?' she answered facetiously and with a wry grin.

Anna's furrowed brows became smooth again and she responded with a broad smile showing her new dentures in all their glory.

'Your teeth look really good Anna, so shiny and clean!' remarked Fiona as they laughed together relaxing in each other's company once more. Having taken the advice of her long term dentist, Anna had decided to have her few remaining teeth removed all in one go and in order to ensure a good fit the new dentures had been pushed into her sore gums before they'd had a chance to heal. This theory had worked remarkably well and Anna's new pearly whites had bedded in to her gums nicely.

Anna smiled as she watched Fiona working the folds of the napkins, as instructed, holding many treasured memories of her as a small child sitting opposite her just as she was now with her golden ringlets and adoring eyes looking up at Anna, full of trust and love.

As she studied her now, her little 'kleine', all grown up, her hair a tawny brown colour, now grown long and thick, she blinked and cleared her throat as nostalgia threatened to engulf her. The moment passed and Anna swallowed hard quickly becoming brusque and businesslike as she hurried her along, 'Good girl, that's right but try to be quick, I need to have one hundred serviettes ready by noon.'

Fiona sighed cheerlessly, 'Ok Anna, but truthfully, I did see a tunnel, in the darkness, right at the far corner of the cellar. Do you know where it goes?'

Anna paused for a moment and gave Fiona her full attention.

'Hmm, well, since you ask, I did hear that there was a tunnel there once but it was all blocked up years ago. I don't think there's anything there now.   The monks from the old monastery used to use it, so I believe, they stored their wine down there in the cellar probably hundreds of years ago, hmm yes' she nodded, 'well that's what I heard anyway.'

'Really', encouraged Fiona animated, as Anna then leant forward and whispered almost conspiratorially;

'I also heard that a number of catholic priests might have used it as an escape route during the dissolution of the monasteries. There now Fiona, are you happy with my little stories', she chuckled and sighed,

'Aaah, my little liebchen, I'm sure there are many stories to be told about all sorts of 'goings on' in this place over the ages. This building probably holds many secrets!'

Fiona gave a wide smile of pleasure at this new found discovery and felt quite excited by these possible explanations. She decided there and then to delve a little deeper into the mystery of the monks and the catholic priests.

Chapter Two:

Vera was the quiet waitress who looked after 'the well', a short woman with a slightly stooped demeanour and reddish hair which was regularly tinted, probably too often, to cover up the grey. She had three thoughtless self-centred sons and a husband who had left them all long ago. Sometimes she would sneak her family in to her dining room and feed them all without anyone knowing. The restaurant was so busy and receipts were rarely checked it could be done quite easily; the trusting nature of the owners could be abused if there was a willingness to do it.

'The well' was a smaller dining room compared to Anna's, given its name because it was on a lower level and accessed down three narrow steps at the corner of the room. There were only a dozen or so small tables in Vera's room, some for four, and some for a cosy twosome. Although this room was not as popular as Anna's (some customers would book well in advance for that pleasure) those shoppers who just wanted to pop in out of the rain for a quiet cup of tea or coffee found Vera's room warm and welcoming.

Above the well there was a dining room nicknamed the long room, this was a long narrow room with tables abutted to the walls on either side of the room with a walkway in the middle. The long room was looked after by Irish Sheelagh, a fun-loving woman with big bosoms and a beehive hair-do who regularly embarrassed Fiona with her loud laughter and intimate questions;

'Where's your boyfriend then, haven't you found one yet?' she'd ask whilst giving her an enormous bear hug as she tore into peals of noisy raucous laughter whilst Fiona's face turned various shades of crimson red.

Fiona always felt quite daunted whenever she was sent on an errand to the long room. It was accessed via the busy landing above the shop, where thronging customers buzzed around the coat rack like bees around a honey pot, whilst others hovered nearby in the queue, impatiently idle while they waited to be seated. The booking area just around the corner was often blocked by big bottomed waitresses taking table reservations over the phone and Fiona would need to negotiate gingerly around them before she eventually reached the head of the long room.

Just as she arrived a sea of chattering faces would suddenly, almost uniformly, turn to look in her direction, many of them regulars as they nodded and smiled in recognition, watching her progress along the narrow walkway between the tables. Her goal, at the far end of the room was a large antique welsh dresser where she would self-consciously refill a sauce jar, collect more cutlery, or complete the errand she'd been sent to do and then she would have the long walk back again.

If possible in order to avoid the long embarrassing walk she would prefer to approach the long room via the courtyard garden which would lessen the impact of her entrance as she could sidle in through the French doors. She could only do this if the weather was good and 'Ching' was chained up.

Ching was her Grandmother's dog, bred for his looks, and there was no doubt Ching was a strikingly beautiful crossbreed, part 'Chow' from Northern China. The local name for the breed was 'Songshi Quan' meaning 'puffy lion dog', and of course the name was extremely apt. A striking shade of golden-brown, his coat was long and thick and resembled a round ball of soft fluff tempting enough to bury one's face in and poking out of it a black pointed nose and small dark velvet ears, which were always razor sharp and alert. Unfortunately his vicious nature, snarling teeth and lifeless eyes ensured Fiona steered well clear of him.

Winifred Fordham, Fiona's Grandmother, appeared to have a fondness for collecting waifs and strays. She'd offered to take Ching from one of her 'bingo' friends who'd found him difficult to handle and Win had just brought him home one night after the club much to George's chagrin. Another time she'd purchased a small Capuchin monkey at a London market, again on a bit of a whim. He'd arrived at the restaurant wearing a tiny crimson fez with yellow piping and tassel and a little waistcoat to match. The little creature, wild and confused, was often left alone upstairs on a long leash and would amuse himself by leaping from chair to chair in the sitting room. Sadly he only lived for just over a year as patently the restaurant was not a conducive environment for such a feral pet.

Another even more unusual member of Nana Win's collection of strays over the years was taken in just after Fiona had been born, and his name was Alf!

The story Fiona had been told about Alf was always a little unclear. She had never been quite sure who he was or why he was there, but he lived amongst the family and had a small bedroom opposite the attic on the top floor, two doors down from her own. He didn't speak very much and used to shuffle along the corridors like an old man, although intriguingly Fiona didn't think he was that old.

His second-hand attire was always a little shabby and too big for him, his baggy trousers hitched up with an old belt, and he always wore a hat, either a flat cap or a beret. Fiona couldn't remember ever seeing him without his hat on. He seemed to be a sort of odd job man who carried out mundane tasks for her Grandmother, such as sweeping and cleaning and he would sometimes go out on small shopping errands in the town.

Whenever she mentioned Alf to her mother or father, they would brush the conversation aside with disinterest and the most she had ever learned about him was that her Grandmother had taken pity on him many years before and had, quite literally, taken him in. Fiona was apprehensive about him being there. She felt he didn't belong and thought it must be a very lonely existence for him. He never appeared to have any family or friends visit him and she imagined him sitting alone in his room during the evenings with just his small black and white television for company. She often wondered whether he had a family somewhere who were missing him and wondering where he was.

Chapter Three:

Fiona's room was right at the top of the building on the second floor almost in the eaves. The stairs up to the top landing were very narrow and would often creak with age. A thin spindly banister rail led up to the small landing and once at the top it was possible to lean right over and look down, past the first floor and further, right down to the very bottom level so that the top of the wide steps at the shop could be seen.

As a small child, Fiona had never wanted to go to bed at night, the creaking of the floorboards and the noises in the rafters would keep her awake and even when she had fallen asleep, she would often wake up, calling out to her mother that she'd had a bad dream, or that someone had been in her room, leaning over her. Her mother had always managed to coax her back to bed telling her not to be so silly and eventually she would drift off back to sleep again.

The large draughty attic on the same floor could be found at the top of three dusty wooden steps hidden behind a black wooden door. The door had been heavily painted with many layers over the years and was set flush within the uneven bulbous wall. Sometimes when she was younger and her school friends had come to play, she would enjoy showing them the 'scary' attic full of junk; old mirrors, bookcases, cupboards, and piles of dusty old books and she would watch their wonder and admiration as they uttered expletives;

'Wow! Cor you're so lucky living in a place like this.'

But actually she didn't like to go in the attic on her own very much. There was always a cold wind blowing, largely because one of the broken windows had been patched up roughly with some old tape and the sound it made as it blew through the gaping hole was akin to a whining, wailing voice which she felt, in her vivid imagination, was warning her to stay away.

Fiona's bedroom was situated at the far end of the top floor landing, and was literally in the rafters. The ceilings were sloped and her mother had done a grand job of painting all the walls and ceilings in a whitewash paint which threw into stark comparison the myriad dark wooden beams running at various angles to one another. On one half of the ceiling in Fiona's room, which she shared with her sister Caroline, Jean's artistic brother Bert from Kent had lovingly drawn giant cartoon characters for the girls when they were younger and the huge shapes of Yogi Bear, Desperate Dan and Tweety Pie stared down at them from the misshapen, bulbous wall above their beds. The middle bedroom was occupied by Jean and Dougie and their two younger children, Helen and Danny.

The third bedroom along, and directly opposite the attic, belonged to Alf.

One morning Fiona had been walking past his room on her way downstairs when she noticed his door had been left slightly ajar. On any other day she would not have bothered about it but on this particular day, for some reason and she couldn't explain why, her curiosity overcame her and she looked through the opening to see that the room was empty. She looked about her and moving forward quietly and carefully she pushed the door open a little to see into the room.

As she entered the room she saw that behind the door on the right hand side of the room it was almost completely bare apart from the sparse furniture, a tidily made bed, a chair, and a pair of brown leather slippers placed neatly on the floor at the base of the bed. Fiona's eyes were drawn to the other side of the room, to the corner by the window, where she noticed many pictures on the wall and a shelf full of ornaments. Moving nearer, she saw that they were all of religious significance. She had not thought Alf to be a religious man, but then of course, she realised, that actually she knew nothing about him at all. There were many pictures of Christ and also of the Virgin Mary holding Christ as a child. A strange pungent smell was coming from an oil lamp hanging over the table, upon which was an unusual ornate bible. There were crosses everywhere, she noticed, many of which were Palm Sunday crosses which she remembered making at Sunday school once.

'Can I help you?'

Alf's voice sliced into the silence and Fiona spun round in despair. She felt sick at being discovered, she shouldn't have been in his room and she tried to think of an excuse for being there.

'I'm sorry' she said eventually, 'I saw your door was open and I thought I heard something so I just thought I'd come and ....' her lame apology trailed off into silence as Alf came forwards into the room. He shut the door behind him and walked slowly towards the bed. Flushed and embarrassed as she was, she couldn't help noticing how tired and drawn he looked. He looked as though he was carrying the weight of the world on his shoulders and she began to wonder more and more about his past and how he had come to be here. He took off his hat, and she saw that he had slightly unkempt, tousled brown hair.

As he sat down on the bed, he put his cap to one side, and looked up at her in puzzlement.

'What was it that you thought you heard?' he enquired, his brow creasing a little in his confusion.

This was the first time she had openly seen his face, and for any length of time, and she quickly realised with surprise that he was definitely not as old as she had previously thought. There was only a hint of grey at the temples of his otherwise honey streaked brown hair which hung down the sides of his face in a gentle wave. His countenance was a little lined and tanned but that was not surprising as he worked outside a great deal, his features were not unpleasant, his nose was fine and straight, and indeed his skin had an almost youthful quality.

Fiona began to feel a strange sense of disconnection between them as she continued to study him and realised he was not looking at her but seemingly straight through her. His eyes had a fixed, faraway look and she noticed for the first time that their colour was of the most piercing, pale ice blue it almost took her breath away. As he fixed his gaze on her again, taking in her casual garb of blue bell-bottomed jeans and embroidered cheesecloth blouse, she began to feel extremely uncomfortable.   Realising she had flagrantly invaded his privacy she broke away from his gaze and looked towards the door, carefully edging her way towards it.

'I'm so sorry' she said again, fumbling with the door knob, which rattled but didn't turn and for a brief fearful moment the thought crossed her mind that he might have locked it but eventually the door opened and she quickly made her escape.

Once she was back in her room she sank down on the floor leaning against the door and quietly sat there for a good while thinking about what she had seen. Her heart was still racing but she wasn't quite sure why. He was a nobody, he wasn't even family, why should she be worried about what he thought and yet she felt that somehow she had crossed a forbidden line, something had changed and she didn't yet know what it was.

Chapter Four:

Winifred Fordham was a hard worker. Every day, at 6 am she awoke, and before she rose from her bed, her mind would click into action mentally sorting the priority order for the day's chores. She was driven to keep on top of what had to be done, she would not let the customers down, and had long ago realised that the only way to run a successful business was to keep the customers happy. She would never let anything distract her from that goal, not her children, or her grandchildren and in a sometimes disrespectful manner, her husband!

Win had met George in London when she was in service as a chambermaid in a grand house in Regent Street where she had learned her trade and how to graft.

It was not long after the Great War when many girls like Win had arrived from small towns and villages travelling in to London to find work. Once they had alighted from the charabancs these innocents realised almost immediately that London was a totally different world to the one they had left. It could have been a million miles away from the quiet tranquil countryside where they'd grown up. They had been used to seeing the odd horse and cart on their local roads, but now, here in the city, it was bustling. There were noisy cars, trams and underground trains, and even just crossing the road became a risky business.

Once employment had been found, and the long, arduous shifts completed, all the girls had to think about then was going out and having fun, out into the town's bars and cafés they would go, large groups of them, meeting up with boys, and those long hours spent at the work place became secondary. But Win was different; she still enjoyed going out into town now and again and having fun but she had her head screwed on, she saw this new adventure as an opportunity not to be missed, and she would always put work first. As a reliable member of staff, she was always ready to do extra shifts or lend a hand if help was needed.

One evening the butler asked her if she'd mind staying in one night and working a bit of overtime. He explained to her that a surprise guest was coming to stay but it was all very secret and she was not to say a word. She readily agreed and the next morning she was the first one up to prepare and serve breakfast to the visitor.

Her reward for this additional duty involved great surprise and excitement when she found out that the visitor was none other than the Prince of Wales! She had not been fazed by it at all, in fact she'd loved it, rising to the challenge, bowing and curtseying for all she was worth.

After that first tantalising taste of grandeur she believed she could achieve anything in life. In fact in observing the Prince in all his finery she realised she wanted more, a lot more.

George was just 15 when he'd lied about his age and signed up with the Hampshire regiment, he'd served in Belfast until he was discharged in 1919 glad to have been returned whole with all his arms and legs intact after the horrors he'd seen, and he considered himself a very lucky man.

Deciding that he liked the discipline of army life he joined the Household Cavalry (the Blues), a regiment solely responsible for the protection of the Queen and visiting dignitaries. It was on that very same day when they happened to be accompanying HRH Prince Edward, the Prince of Wales, escorting his carriage back to the Palace, that he spied the little chamber maid at the door of the great house.

As he caught her eye he bowed his head almost imperceptibly to anyone else but Win had seen it and she smiled blushing encouragingly when he returned her smile. He cut a dashing figure, as he sat astride his beautifully groomed horse, striking in his smart blue jacket, white trousers and shiny black boots.

Once the Prince was safely secreted within his carriage she watched the handsome guard's red plume fluttering gently in the breeze atop his shiny silver helmet as they moved away. Win thought to herself, yes, he'll do very nicely.

Win and George were married in London during the great depression of the early 1930s. Although times were hard to begin with Win's experience in the hospitality trade paid off when they decided to start a business together as publicans. Their first pub was 'The Westmoreland Arms' in Shoreditch in London. They did very well for a few years and were busy every night; even on that desperate night in 1939 when World War Two broke out the pub seemed busier than normal. Stoic in adversity, the couple continued trading.

Even though the pub was situated right in the middle of the London blitz and under regular attack from the German Luftwaffe, night after night they continued to be full to the rafters. Human nature, they'd come to realise, particularly during the years of the depression, was such that no matter what was going on around them, folks would still find solace outside their own homes, would seek to socialise with friends and lovers, have a good time, get drunk, laugh and be merry, and try to forget about tomorrow's bad news.

Drinking was the antidote to misery.

And so Win and George carried on through the war and enough money was made to enable them to buy two more pubs; The Queens Head at Titchfield and The King's Head in Fareham. Members of the family were put in as managers, George's sister Evelyn in one and Win's brother Harry in the other.

The pub line continued going from strength to strength until a string of no less than four pubs were held and managed by the family and a lot of money was being made.

Fiona had seen old photos of Nana Win wearing furs and the finest couture at the height of their success and also of Grandad George sitting at one end of the bar with a drink in one hand, a cigar in the other, holding court, and enjoying his stately position. Four healthy sons were born to them during this time; Ronnie, Jack, Dougie and Billy.

After a few years in the pub trade Grandad George was beginning to feel idle. He decided he needed something else to do. The pubs were running themselves pretty much on their own and all he had to do was prop up the bar on occasion and chat with the regulars.

He had been given the nod by an acquaintance that a bookmakers' business in the local area was up for grabs.

'It's a sure cert', advised the guy enthusiastically.

George went to see Win.

'I'm bored Win', he explained 'you're so busy with the boys and the business; I'd like to have a go, you know, do something on my own, see if I can make a success of it!'

At first Win laughed at him, not willing to let go of the purse strings, but this was the first time he had ever asked anything of her and so later, when he came to her again with a grave, hangdog expression, she agreed to his request with good grace, indulging him in his whimsy, blissfully ignorant of any real concern or possible repercussions.

George managed to set up his new business in pretty quick fashion and all seemed to be going well and, with his bank account balance rising steadily, he felt quite proud of himself.

Sadly this happy state of affairs was not to last. One fateful day a large number of punters had been tipped off and arrived to place bets on an outsider they knew had already crossed the finishing line and won the race! The information had not come through to the betting shop in time and all the windows had been busy and many bets placed!

When the betting slips came in George had not initially realised the consequences but pretty soon he became aware of the numbers involved and the tally and that all the claims were valid and so he had no alternative but to go cap in hand to Win and confess the impending disaster.

Together, they soon comprehended that the debt was insurmountable. They had no choice. The pubs would have to be sold off to pay off George's creditors.

Win was distraught, disappointed and so unspeakably angry with George that she could hardly look at him.

The futility and waste of all that hard work was hard to bare and when she'd finally finished berating him she ceaselessly continued to blame herself for her thoughtlessness.

'I'm so sorry, Win' George sobbed as he knelt down in front of her, surrounding her ample waist with his strong arms, 'please forgive me, I promise I'll make it up to you' he begged.

She looked down at him and his now badly balding head. He was hugging and imploring her as though she were his mother and instinctively she lifted her own soft chubby arms to comfort him and soothe him as she would a child, but something seemed to switch off inside her, her heart lay like a dead weight in her chest, and she lowered them again with both fists clenched very tightly in two round balls of unforgiving rage.

Luckily Win was not dim-witted. She was canny and had been prudent enough to put away some of her own savings in a separate account and they were able to scrape together enough money to buy a small sweet shop in Soham, her home town, and so the whole family moved out of London and back to Soham where they all lived quite happily for three years. Well, almost all family members were reasonably content, except Win of course. The driving force in her life was still money, the luxury it could provide and the status within society and gradually and carefully she managed to claw her way back up life's ladder saving every penny she could until there were sufficient funds in the bank to purchase one more public house in Dartford called the 'The Bull's Head.'

Uprooted once again from Soham to Dartford, the family enjoyed life in the busy thriving town not far from the Thames where they did very well for about five years, and, as the boys became men, they too supported their parents and earned their keep serving behind the bar.

It transpired however that during the fifties times were changing for the pub trade. It appeared that televisions were now taking a corner place in many a sitting room across the country and encroaching on people's leisure time. Previous pub goers were now staying in and watching TV in the evenings.

Shrewdly Win sensed the change coming. Her foresight and keen business sense had always taught her to remain ahead of the game and to be prepared to cut losses. She persuaded

George that they should now change direction and go into the restaurant trade instead which was now up and coming.

'It will just be for lunches and afternoon teas' she told him, 'with perhaps a bit of home-made cake and coffee served in the mornings, and', she added emphatically, 'we will not be serving any alcohol!'

Win had finally come to realise that she'd had her fill of 'last orders', and 'time' and the often unpleasant but always necessary 'chucking out' session which happened late at night for those who didn't want to go home or maybe didn't have a home to go to! She wasn't young any more and the temptation of a quieter life beckoned.

And so, yet again, the family upped sticks and moved to St Albans, in Hertfordshire, and to 'The Pilgrims Rest' at Number One Holywell Hill.

George did not quibble over the decision and to be honest he wouldn't have been listened to even if he had. The gnawing guilt he felt after losing so much money was always with him and with his tail between his legs he did as he was told with no option but to follow Win's lead and try to help her make a success of this new business idea.

Win was not completely oblivious to his capitulation but her trust in him was gone and she didn't know if it would ever come back again. She knew she couldn't let him make the business decisions anymore and it seemed, whether she liked it or not, she wore the trousers now.

She loved him, as much as she could ever love anyone, but she always felt alone, as though no one really understood her. Her emotions were kept private, locked away, there was no soft side. She had to be tough. She loved George and the boys of course, in her own way, but from a distance. She could never let any of them get in her way. Her goal was to keep the customers happy, to keep them coming in, and in her heart and soul they would always take priority.

Win also knew it was important to keep up appearances in front of the staff and the customers and her own facade was very important to her, it was her protective shield, and she always took a pride in it.

Her classic clothing and make-up were always carefully chosen to impress. Her hair, a soft light brown colour, was regularly permed and tinted and she applied a thick beige foundation daily with matching face powder to cover her worst features, a large roman nose and a slightly pointed chin.

With one or even three rows of expensive pearls fastened securely round her now slightly saggy neck and the swift application of bold red lipstick to her rather unremarkable lips she was ready for battle and for the busy day ahead. Win was a small woman, only a smidgen above five feet, but she could match the strength and energy of any man.

Chapter Five:

As time moved on Grandad George decided that in fact he quite liked his new life in St Albans. The restaurant was doing well and he could enjoy the trappings of wealth without the responsibility. He was a big man in stature as well as in the community and would often meet up with other businessmen in the town and sit drinking with them at his favourite watering hole, The Peahen Hotel, right next door to the restaurant at the very top of Holywell Hill.

Occasionally Fiona would be asked to pop next door to the Peahen lounge bar to ask Grandad George a question or perhaps to call him back for something;

'Go ask Grandad next door where he left the cheque for the greengrocer?'

Or on another day,

'Go tell Grandad the Butcher's here?'

She would agree to go a little reluctantly because the bar was mainly a male environment, forbidden territory for a young girl, but on the other hand she quite liked the notion.

As she shyly poked her head round the door of the Peahen to look for him, he would spy her and tipsily call her over to his table, proceeding to proudly show off his 'beautiful grand-daughter' to his drinking chums.

'Come and sit down here next to me', he would call out to her and after she'd obediently sat down he would hug her to him joyfully, rough and hard, while his fellow drinkers raised their glasses and laughed along with him in a patronising humour, relishing her youthful embarrassment.

Within the hierarchy of the town George was thought of quite highly but when away from listening ears he would always admit quietly to her, 'Yes, yes I suppose I do alright here, they all seem to like me well enough, but I'm no 'tub thumper' and they don't like that. I won't change though, no matter what their enticements might be.'

George remained the visible figurehead of the business, always involved in any family discussions about customer numbers, pricing, or staffing, but Fiona knew this was all a facade and it was evident to her that the real driving force behind the business was her Nana Win.

As Fiona grew older she considered herself duty bound to help out in the restaurant when required but she was always willing enough. She could wait on tables in any of the dining rooms, or work on the small till in the shop, or wash up in the scullery. There was no question of refusing especially if they were short-staffed. It was an expectation that all family members could be relied upon in any emergency situation.

She regularly helped with the washing up in the scullery at the far end of the kitchen.

The scullery was a dark, damp area where three white stone sinks, square and deep, were aligned side by side in front of the sash windows. Each sink was connected to the next with a large wooden draining board in between which then joined at the walls on either side. Countless pots, pans and paraphernalia were stored in the old cupboards and shelves which ran along the length of the other walls.

Fiona would stand in idle chatter with her father in the mornings watching him as he bent busily over the corner sink, washing and chopping cabbage after cabbage, every single morning of every single day, seven days a week, and always with urgency as though time was against him which indeed it was because there was always another chore waiting, needing to be done.

Every item used in the restaurant; crockery, cutlery, glasses, pots, pans, were all washed and dried by hand, a constant, never-ending stream of trays coming through to the scullery until the lunchtime rush was over when there would be a short respite mid afternoon. During that short spell everyone stood around, leaning against the sinks and draining boards, tea towels in hand, chatting, laughing, and enjoying those few quiet moments until the afternoon teas began and another surge of crockery traffic would arrive, trailing off again at around 6 o'clock when it would all be over for another day.

The scullery was always shrouded in darkness due to the miniscule amount of light allowed to shine in via three sash windows at the back of the room behind the sinks. On a bright day dusty beams of light would endeavour to probe the broken blinds but the corrugated iron roof outside, old and peppered with rust holes, was a barrier to any brightness coming through.

This dank dark area outside was used for storing heaps of large sacks containing sprouts, potatoes, carrots and other vegetables and was also a pathway to the men's toilets. This gave customers the opportunity to peer inside inquisitively on their way past.

A second storey which ran along the length of the kitchen and finished above the scullery contained the reasonably comfortable living quarters where Fiona and her siblings, Caroline, Helen and Danny, lived for many years playing happily together while the grown-ups were at work downstairs. This apartment was known as the flat.

At the far end of the flat was a quirkily unusual bathroom.

Due to the age of the building the floor level at this end was extremely haphazard and there was a sharp slant downwards.

When Fiona was a child and at a certain time every Saturday morning she would rush into the sloping bathroom, lift the heavy trap door partially enclosed by a small wooden fence and with great effort would kneel precariously whilst holding it aloft using the brass ring handle. A cacophony of noise and warmth would always rush up from below anointing her face with a golden glow as she peered down the row of plank-like steps into the scullery.

She was not allowed to come down these steps although she had tried to do this once but had been scolded sharply to go straight back up. However she was able to call out to her father while he stood at his usual spot stooped over the corner sink as he washed and noisily chopped the cabbage on the wooden draining board and he would hear her call down to him,

'Daddy, daddy, it's Thunderbirds on the telly!'

He would then quickly walk over to the bottom of the steps and look up at her with a smile on his face.

'OK, I'll be up in a minute, go back now, there's a good girl.'

At the time he would mean it but very often he never came. He always wanted to, to sit upstairs snuggled up with his daughters and watch Thunderbirds, but there was always too much to do.

Fiona would shut the trap door carefully and return to the flat where her younger sister was waiting for her and they would cuddle up and watch television together or sit and do puzzles at the small table by the window.

Together they would play with their toy record player and lay on their tummies on the floor whilst listening to the small brightly coloured discs; 'Let him go, let him tarry' was their favourite.

'Let him go, let him tarry, let him sink or let him swim,
He doesn't care for me and I don't care for him
He can go and get another that I hope he will enjoy
For I'm going to marry a far nicer boy'

Sometimes they would sing and dance around together holding hands and keeping each other company, happy knowing that their parents weren't far away.

Chapter Six:

Fiona finally became a paid employee at the restaurant in her mid teens and every Saturday afternoon at around three in the afternoon she would arrive at the scullery to start washing and drying the dishes until around six o'clock for the handsome sum of three pounds! She wasn't alone in her work as local boys, Richard and Ian, similar in age to Fiona, would also come in to help and earn a bit of extra cash.

She decided fairly soon after meeting him that she loved Richard passionately although he didn't know it, or pretended not to, but he was her first yearning, the first boy who'd sent her pulses racing. Every time their hands accidentally touched in the soap suds her heart would beat so loud and fast she thought he must be able to hear it. But he never asked her out, never showed her the slightest interest, in that respect anyway. He would contentedly chat with her and laugh at her jokes but no more than that.

It was Ian who showed more interest. She knew Ian fancied her, she could tell.

He tried to kiss her once. His soap covered hands carefully placed either side of her, blocking her exit, while she stood tea-towel in hand and trapped prey-like between the sinks and the table. To her dismay as she backed right up against the wall he leant forward, his intention obvious, and in her desperate need to escape she bobbed down so quickly that he ended up plonking a big wet kiss right in the middle of her left eye which was excruciatingly embarrassing but quite comical at the same time and they both almost choked with laughter. He took the hint though, on that day anyway, but always waiting for another opportunity.

Washing and drying hundreds of plates was an arduous monotonous task every week and so in order to help them get through the long hours they would often turn on the radio and sing along to the charts. Ian enjoyed listening to her soulful voice as she sang with the Supremes one minute and Cockney Rebel the next and she was flattered when he asked her many times to join his band.

'Please' he cajoled, 'you have a beautiful singing voice. 'Why don't you just come along and try it, you never know you might enjoy yourself,' he was constantly trying to persuade her. There was no doubt she was tempted, a part of her really wanted to do it but she continued to turn him down every time, partly because she was nervous about singing in front of an audience but also she didn't want to encourage him. Ian was covered in orange freckles, jolly and friendly enough and she did enjoy his company, but her heart didn't beat for him like it did for Richard.

Every Saturday evening once the restaurant had closed, the ritual handing out of the wages took place.

George enjoyed his role as the grand benefactor and always made an impressive entrance parading into the kitchen at the end of the day like a drill sergeant. He'd balance, within his broad arms, the heavy till drawer always overflowing with cash from the busy day's takings. He'd sit ceremoniously at the head of the kitchen table and carefully position small piles of coins ready for the casual staff to come and collect one by one. Fiona received no special treatment and would have to stand in the queue with the rest of the staff to wait her turn. When she arrived at the front of the queue, George would beckon her forward to receive her money, and strangely she always had to resist a bizarre compulsion to bob a little curtsey!

George would enjoy teasing her and pretend that he wasn't going to pay her. He loved to have his little joke at the expense of others but not in an unkindly way and she indulged him along with the others, after all he was the boss!

When she was a small child he would often grab her and cuddle her, squeezing her so tight that she thought she might faint, and then he would pinch her nose between the knuckles of his two fingers, before releasing her suddenly and pretending he had stolen it. And there, lo and behold, it was to be seen sitting between his fingers! Of course it was only his thumb poking through, which was always pretty obvious to Fiona, but every time he played this little prank he would roar with laughter as though it were the first time and eventually she learnt to endure the small amount of pain she received in payment for his grandfatherly enjoyment!

George loved to travel abroad but Win never went with him. Her obsession for work and lack of trust in everyone around her meant that he was forced to holiday alone. George never complained. He would set off happily to join a cruise ship sailing from Southampton to the island of Madeira, a favourite destination of his. On one visit he had purchased a beautiful antique mandolin and brought it back with him as a present for Fiona.

'The sun shines every day,' he told her, 'there is no winter, only warmth,' and he proudly boasted of the wonderful flower festival which took place every year in April in the capital city of Funchal!

'Ah Fiona you have never seen flowers like it,' he embellished further, 'huge blooms, in abundance, they blossom all year round you know; everywhere on the island, and you observe that the harbour at Funchal is naturally protected by spectacular mountains. I can see their peaks rise majestically up to the sky and, as I hang on to the ship's rail, I can see a kaleidoscope of colours from quite a distance and the aroma is divine, it engulfs you, even as you are coming in to dock at the harbour. It is a truly splendid place!' he asserted.

She believed him and knew that this was her Grandfather's own private Shangri-La and she made him a promise that one day she would go and see it for herself.

Secretly Win was quite glad when George was gone. In a rather cruel way that was one less disturbance she'd have to deal with for two weeks anyway. She always wanted to focus on the matter in hand and was never one for distractions, gossip or silly jokes. Sadly her life had not gone the way she'd planned and there had been some disappointments along the way.

The loss of the pubs had been a huge setback for her but she'd managed to put that behind her and on the whole she was happy with the new business and tried not to dwell on past mistakes. However a great sadness for Win, and one that she had only superficially managed to suppress, was that her darling baby girl, Elizabeth, her one and only daughter born after four healthy sons had not survived beyond two days. The loss of Elizabeth had changed Win forever.

At the time she'd succumbed to a despair not overcome easily and it had been many months before she'd stopped feeling numb and the empty feeling inside her gradually decreased. She was alone in her grief, of that she was sure. No one could ever understand her pain.

She decided from then on, for her own survival, she needed to conquer those emotions and negative feelings. They made her vulnerable and so she needed to be able to switch them off! Surprisingly she found this ability became easier over time until the talent of blocking her emotions almost at will became second nature to her. Another important part of this philosophy of survival against pain was to always remain busy.

On the day Win had found Alf in the alleyway she had been outside in the courtyard garden checking on the plants and enjoying the sunshine.

She discovered that gardening definitely soothed her soul and took great pleasure in feeding and watering the new standard roses she'd recently planted in one of the raised beds. It had cheered her to see the profusion of pink buds on each one which would make a fine display to please the customers as they walked through.

As she stood back to admire her work she heard a prolonged whimpering sound coming from the alley way behind her but she was not sure whether it was animal or human. She turned and listened for a moment and then started to walk slowly down the crazy-paved pathway towards the gate. She stopped at the gate and opened it slightly, looking to her right and to where the pitiful noise was coming from.

There she spied him in the shadows, crouched under the archway, in peculiar clothing, his eyes wide and staring, as if he had been scared out of his wits. At first she thought he might be drunk and was of a mind to drive him off but when she saw he was only a youngish lad she moved quietly towards him not wanting to frighten him using gentle soothing sounds to keep him calm.

He was shivering with cold and mumbling incoherently, using words Win did not understand, and she had supposed at the time that he might be foreign. She considered he could not have been more than about sixteen years old.

Win quickly fetched a warm blanket and then returned to him again with a mug of warm milk which he drank thirstily.

Gaining his trust a little she tried to convince him to come inside to safety.

'Come, come with me', she'd coaxed 'I won't hurt you, I promise', and Alf had clung to her in fear, realising this woman who had taken pity on him was his life line, his sanctuary.

The police were called to the restaurant but they did not seem very interested at the time. They construed his name to be Alfred and a few enquiries were made but there had been no missing person reported in the area and Alfred appeared strangely content to stay in this safe haven he had found.

Win told the police she was happy for him to remain with her, at least for a while, and as she watched over him, protectively, over the next few days and weeks a strange feeling began to stir within her.

There was something about this young lad, his desperate need for compassion, the aura of loss and sadness surrounding him, which she recognised as far worse than anything she might have suffered. She wondered what on earth he had been through in his short life that had made him fear everything and everyone around him.

The profound knowledge that his need was far greater than her own had started to fill the empty void inside of her and she began to understand how human emotions of pity, love, sadness and grief, although painful at times, are an important part of life, they make us who we are, and should not be shunned or shut down and it is only indifference we should fear as the catalyst for all hope being lost.

Chapter Seven:

After the incident in Alf's bedroom, Fiona had avoided him as much as possible. He didn't appear to have mentioned it to anyone else and so life continued much as it had before.

Due to staff holidays Fiona was asked to help out with a bit of waitressing in the shop. She knew full well she wasn't the best waitress in the world but she entered into the role with gusto and verve, her forgetfulness and youthful clumsiness readily forgiven by the customers, in exchange for her bright personality and willingness to learn.

The shop was an invitingly bright reception area receiving a large amount of natural light from the road outside. It was accessed by the main front door and on a cold day it could be quite draughty but the burnished oak panelling and polished parquet flooring gave it a warm ambience. Pew-like tables were positioned around the walls enabling customers to get a good view of Holywell Hill where they could observe the comings and goings of passers by and watch the slow moving traffic as it trundled up the hill to the main part of town.

Saturdays and Sundays were always the busiest days and a queue of patient diners would form across the middle of the shop and up the five wide steps to the small landing waiting for a table to become free. Above the entrance was a large swinging sign emblazoned in gold calligraphic font with the words 'The Pilgrims Rest' and depicting a priest-like pilgrim wearing a long dark cloak, sitting astride his horse and carrying a staff.

Just inside the window, on a polished wooden shelf, was exhibited a large display of home made cakes; scones, rock cakes, apple pie squares, and mince pies, all piled precariously high on the expansive china plates, enticing people in for a quick purchase before they continued on their way home down the hill.

The cash register could be found in the corner of the shop tucked away enabling people to pop in quickly to purchase a few cakes or for diners to settle their bill on the way out. All these comings and goings ensured that the shop was indeed a consistently busy, bustling area.

The entire restaurant, including Anna's room, Vera's room, the shop and the long room, could seat a hundred people and was often full without a table free. It was situated at the top of the legendary Holywell Hill in Saint Albans which had been given its religious name by Christian pilgrims during their early visits to the site of the 'holy well', which had sprung up miraculously at the top of the hill during the beheading of Albanus during the third century AD. Albanus or Saint Alban as he was now known had been honoured ever since as the first Christian martyr in England.

Over hundreds of years right up to the present day enthusiastic visitors from near and far had continued to flock to the Abbey to see the shrine of Saint Alban and many would seek out the restaurant for a welcome pot of tea or coffee, perhaps savouring one of the reputedly scrumptious scones.

The Pilgrims Rest was indeed a sanctuary for certain regular customers such as Mr Atkins the assistant bank manager from Barclays.

He always arrived promptly every morning at 11 am, smartly dressed in his pin-striped suit, a morning paper tucked under his arm, his reading glasses at the ready. He looked forward to his mid-morning cup of coffee at his favourite table, a small table for two, tucked into the far corner, reserved for his daily visit.

With only half an eye on his paper he would secretly observe the comings and goings of the busy shop and watch the outside world go by through the generous window as he slowly sipped his coffee, reflecting on his life and how and why it had all gone so dreadfully wrong.

Unhappily, following marital harmony of thirty years, his wife's sudden desertion into the brawny arms of the local swimming instructor had left him reeling for several months, but now subsequently he just felt numb and the daily regimented routine offered him some small reason to live.

An unfortunate elderly couple found safe haven every Thursday lunchtime accompanied by their forty year old son who suffered from a neurological condition present since birth. He would utter random guttural sounds including belching loudly and then afterwards smile widely pulling back his lips with his stubby fingers showing off his gappy tombstone teeth. Most customers smiled sympathetically or just pretended not to notice.

On Tuesdays, Ted the dustman arrived with his 'friend' Malcolm in tow, a comical couple who always caused a bit of a stir. Malcolm had explained to one of the waitresses once, in secretive hushed tones, that his job was to wash dead bodies at the morgue! The two of them would sit chatting together whilst eating their lunch and then afterwards they would reach into their bags and pull out their needlework continuing to sew happily together for an hour or more.

A regular customer, known as leather jacket, caused utter confusion one day when he ordered an 'Adam's Ale' with his meal. The waitress quickly apologised to him explaining that she was very sorry but alcohol was not served at the Pilgrims Rest and then he'd laughed at her whilst clearing up his little foible by saying that it was just a glass of water he was after!

A lamentable occasion had occurred when an ill-fated customer had suffered a seizure during his meal on a particularly busy day when Win had been serving in the shop. Of course she did the right thing and quickly rang for the ambulance but deciding there was nothing more she could do for the poor chap she continued serving lunches, undaunted, carefully stepping over him as the need arose!

Fiona was enjoying a quiet moment, bending over the cake display in the shop window to retrieve a wayward scone which she'd noticed had fallen off one of the plates and she happened to gaze outside.

As she looked across the road she was surprised to see Alf entering the tobacconist's shop directly opposite.   She watched for a while as he stood waiting in front of the sweet counter.

She could see he was alone in the shop and decided that he appeared rather agitated as he kept looking around furtively.

After a few moments she watched him walk around behind the counter and then disappear from view through a door at the back of the shop.

She was taken aback as she had been in the shop many times before for her father when he'd wanted her to buy him some cigarettes and she'd never noticed it. She wondered why on earth Alf would need to go into the back of the shop!

A voice from behind broke into her reverie,

'Fiona, could I have another coffee,' called Mr Atkins from his corner table.

'Oh, yes, yes, of course,' she responded politely as she walked over to retrieve his empty coffee cup.

She deliberately avoided eye contact following a strange new twinkle she'd noticed in them earlier and so, without looking at him directly, she smiled as she picked up his glass cup and saucer, and sped up the steps along the side passage to the kitchen.

'Another coffee for Mr Atkins' she called out as she walked into the hot steamy buzz of activity.

'Go on then' called out her mother, 'we're a bit busy here dishing up, so you can do it.'

'Oh no, do I have to... Oh, I mean, okay?' sighed Fiona when she saw her Mother's disdainful look, she hated the spitting whistling coffee machine, and it always seemed to splash her whenever she tried to use it.

Luckily, Anna rushed headlong into the kitchen at that particular moment hurrying to get a tray of coffees for her own customers and so she quickly came to Fiona's aid to speed things along.

'Aaah no, no, no, Fiona, you will get it all over yourself if you do it like that, watch me, see you have to put the spout right into the cup like this, so it froths inside the cup and then you won't splash your hand. That's it, right down inside the cup.'

Fiona beamed.   She felt she'd achieved something momentous and proudly presented the freshly brewed frothy coffee to Mr Atkins. 'Thanks, you're a sweetheart', he said, smiling and winking at her. He was enjoying himself so much this morning having Fiona waiting on him - perhaps there was life in the old dog yet, he thought to himself. Fiona moved quickly away, she didn't like the way his eyes kept drifting downwards to the front of her blouse. It made her feel a bit hot and flustered!

The morning passed by swiftly enough but Fiona was curious to know where Alf had disappeared to and what was behind that door? Later on when the lunchtime rush was over and she'd finished serving she went back into the kitchen and spoke to her father lounging in his usual stance against the back door, inhaling and exhaling the cigarette he carefully cradled in his fingers;

'Dad, do you need any more cigarettes?' she asked him cheerily, 'I don't mind popping across the road to the newsagents for you, if you'd like?'

Dougie drew out the slightly crumpled half-empty packet from the depths of his trouser pocket,
'Hmm, well there's still a few in there but I suppose I could do with some for tomorrow….. hang on a minute, what are you doing? You're not supposed to be encouraging me! You're always the one telling me I should give it up?'

Fiona sighed, 'I know Dad, but just think of this as reverse psychology, I'm hoping that if I keep pushing you to buy them eventually you'll reach saturation point and say; no more, no more!' she grinned at him sheepishly.

He gave her a wry smile in return, pretty sure she had some ulterior motive but he handed her a five pound note anyway and watched her as she bounced out of the kitchen calling back to him; 'I'll get ten ok, not twenty!'

She stepped out across the open door next to the ladies toilet and walked into the garden. The glow of the afternoon sun warmed her skin as a bee hummed by on its way to the flower beds. As she skipped down the path to the back gate she was aware of the buzz of conversation and warm laughter coming from the last few customers who were in no hurry to leave after their meal. When she reached the gate she stopped for a moment to make sure nothing was coming up the driveway and then continued on her way downwards under the archway towards the hustle and bustle of Holywell Hill.

Fiona enjoyed the strange atmosphere underneath the cold archway as she walked down the slope and she shivered slightly in the darkness. She sensed dampened memories of days gone by when stage coaches would arrive here for passengers to alight after their long journey from London, stopping off on their way north or perhaps on their return. The rafters above her head were high and dark, made of solid oak beams and even higher above them was further accommodation in the form of an extremely grand room which was her grandparents' sitting room, commonly known as the big room.

As she entered the busy street, she waited for a gap in the traffic and quickly manoeuvred her way across safely. She made her way to the front door of the tobacconist's shop and looked inside. Seeing the shop was empty she entered as quietly as she could and stood examining the wall behind the counter. She realised straight away that the mystery door was secreted in the midst of the wooden panelling and understood immediately why she had never noticed it before.

She stood in silence for a while observing the rows and rows of cigarette packets proudly displayed on the shelves behind the sweet counter?

Her father's favourite was the Players brand with a warning on it saying 'high tar' but he took no notice of any warnings.

If a trailer on television started to warn about the dangers of smoking he'd frantically point to the screen accusingly, demanding loudly 'turn that off?' If no one moved to do his bidding, in the vain hope that he might actually watch it and learn, he'd leap up from his chair and quickly switch it over without delay as if the devil himself was in the room.

Fiona worried about the state of his lungs but acknowledged that his habit had been fixed and formed in his youth during the forties when almost everybody smoked. George, Ronnie and Jean had all indulged but pregnancy had given Jean the opportunity and the reason to kick the habit.   The iconic images of James Dean, Humphrey Bogart and Marlene Dietrich, the epitome of coolness and glamour at the time, promoted the habit as socially attractive and desirable.

Fiona admitted to herself privately that she did quite like the smell of a fresh packet of cigarettes when it had just been opened and the join in the silver wrapping was separated to reveal the 10 or 20 virginal white sticks. She'd often watch her father, curious, when he opened up a new pack. The aroma, like freshly burnt grass, would assail her nostrils in a not unpleasant way. It became almost ceremonial.

He would take a cigarette out of the pack, pat it gently on the back, and then place it between his lips. The match would be struck and then as he lit the tip, she would enjoy watching the intense concentration on his face as he drew in that first long, sweet drag. A few seconds later the distinctive plume of light grey smoke would be exhaled, escaping from his semi-closed lips and simultaneously his large nicotine stained nostrils.

Fiona had found him on his own once enjoying a solitary peaceful smoke in the old upstairs sitting room now standing empty except for one single worn out armchair. He'd made her giggle that day by pursing his lips and blowing out magical smoke circles for her entertainment. She'd watched him in wonder and delight as the circles grew bigger and changed shape as they moved across the room.

She remembered being about eight at the time and had playfully asked him if she could try one of the sticks?

Without hesitation her father had carefully passed the cigarette over to her holding it in front of her mouth while she leaned forward and sucked in! A violent coughing fit had ensued which gradually subsided after a few seconds.

When she'd recovered she expostulated to her father how disgusting it had been. He'd merely smiled knowingly and smugly placed the cigarette back into his mouth. That was exactly the result he'd hoped for; she would never want to smoke a cigarette again. And he was right, she never did.

Fiona tried to position herself so that she was best placed to see what was beyond the door as soon as it was opened.

She rang the bell for service and in a few seconds the door became ajar and the elderly shopkeeper trundled through opening it a little wider. Fiona peered past the smile on Mr Saville's friendly face managing to quickly sketch in her mind quite an imposing room with a remarkably high ceiling and similar décor to that of her grandparent's sitting room, the big room.

However she was taken aback and what really moved her was that the four large sash windows at the back of the room afforded her a wondrous view of the Abbey's grandeur. The sight of it took her breath away and she wondered how she could have missed this incredible outlook during her previous visits to the shop. Unfortunately though, her exploration came to an end as the door began to shut firmly behind the shopkeeper, who politely asked if he could help her.

Chapter Eight:

As Fiona lay in bed that night, she couldn't sleep as she mulled over the day's events. Her sister was staying away with a friend for a few days and so she was alone in the room.

She realised that Alf was becoming an intriguing and mysterious character to her, aware that he was at this very moment sleeping and breathing only a few feet away from her, and yet in reality she knew nothing about him. As she lay there quietly, a slight creak on the stairs made her sit up. She quickly slid out of bed, pulled on her pale blue velvet robe and slipped into her grey satin slippers before carefully peering round the door.

Although it was very dark on the landing area there was a shaft of moonlight from the small window at the top of the stairs. She couldn't see anyone but decided to investigate anyway and made her way carefully along the soft carpeted corridor. She grasped the hand rail and as she looked down over the banisters and into the stairwell she just caught sight of Alf making his way down the second flight of stairs into the restaurant area. She guessed the time must be about two o'clock in the morning and wondered what he was doing up at this hour. Perhaps he couldn't sleep either and was going down to the kitchen to get something to eat or drink? On impulse she decided to follow him.

She looked down at her slippers and quickly returned to her room deciding to slip on her shoes just in case there were any cockroaches about. She'd seen them once before on a late night visit to the kitchen. That time everyone had gone to bed and the kitchen had been shrouded in darkness. She'd reached round to turn on the light before entering and in that instant she'd caught sight of them, hundreds of them, just for a split second or two in the brilliance of the light. They were everywhere, all over the steamers and coffee machines, all along the window ledge, a writhing mass like a secret army covering all the work surfaces. As she stood, frozen to the spot, a multitude of long wavy feelers and yellow eyes turned simultaneously in the direction of the unwanted visitor, and then suddenly they were gone, vanished, back into the crevices and hiding places from whence they'd come! She shivered at the thought.

On reaching the top of the lower staircase she heard the cellar door open and shut and the sound of muffled footsteps descending the cellar stairs. She waited for a moment or two before continuing down to the bottom where she turned the corner and stepped silently up to the cellar door. As she listened, she could hear shoving and pushing sounds down in the cellar and wondered what on earth he was doing down there at this time of night.

Although the cellar was her least favourite place, especially at night and every nerve ending was screaming at her to return to her bed, her curiosity got the better of her and she decided to find out what he was up to.

She carefully opened the door and peered down into the darkness. Slowly and cautiously she descended the dusty wooden steps hanging on to the rail as she went and on reaching the bottom she stood silently for a few seconds on the cold stone floor. The small bulb in the middle of the cellar was aglow throwing eerie shadows against the walls but, as she listened, she could hear nothing.

She looked around and could see that the boxes and tins near the back of the cellar had been moved to one side and there was a dark gap at the corner of the room that she had seen once before. She moved forward stepping carefully to avoid the uneven paving slabs and as she groped her way past the heavy boxes and tins her hand eventually touched the smooth surface of the wall.   It was cold and damp beneath her fingertips and a strange vaporous odour assaulted her nostrils. Fear and dread coursed through her body yet she felt compelled to peer into the darkness. Something was urging her onwards and distant voices echoed all around her. As her eyes grew accustomed to the blackness, she saw, stretching out in front of her a long circular tunnel with a very dim and distant hazy light at the far end. It seemed to beckon her onwards and she started to move cautiously forward.

After she had taken a few steps the pungent smell became very strong and she suddenly felt slightly faint and nauseous. She called out in a small rasping voice 'Alf, Alf, are you there?'

As she clung on to the side of the tunnel wall she began to feel very claustrophobic.   She felt hot and her skin became clammy, her mouth and throat felt parched. As she looked around her the walls started to look uneven with strange shapes, bumps and crevices starting to form whereas before, to her, they had looked smooth. Worse still these undulations seemed suddenly to be taking on the distorted features of human faces. She was mesmerized and realised the faces appeared to be in anguish, like lost souls, trapped. She knew she must be hallucinating, or that it was some kind of optical illusion and so she quickly closed her eyes tight shut.

When she opened them again, the walls appeared smooth once more but the memory of those faces had had a strange effect on her and she was overcome with a dreadful feeling of sadness and despair.

She stumbled on through the tunnel putting her hand out to clutch at the cold clammy wall to steady herself.

In the distance she saw something moving towards her out of the darkness and she could just make out the tall black shape of a hooded figure, a man, wearing a long dark robe.

As he drew near, she sank slowly down to the ground, looking up at the face which appeared above her own, drowning in fathomless depths of icy blue eyes.

As she fainted into grateful oblivion, she was vaguely aware of Alf's voice desperately calling out her name.

****

A few hours later she awoke and lay still for a while feeling disorientated as she tried to get her bearings.   She slowly lifted her heavy head from the pillow and opened her eyes.

Although her vision was a little muzzy she recognised her own wrought iron bedstead and beyond that the sash windows at the far end of the room through which warm dappled light was resting on the pale green carpet.   Someone must have already come in and opened the curtains she thought as her wet brow started to throb painfully and she carefully lowered her head again, closing her eyes for a moment.   She was lying under the covers of her bed but she almost felt as if she were floating above it. Her bedside clock said that it was 8.30 but she decided not to try to get up and so she lay there shaking slightly and feeling quite ill.

There was a knock at the door.

'Come in' Fiona croaked, and Jean's smiling face appeared round the door.

'I've brought you a nice cup of tea' her mother said kindly coming in and calmly putting it on the bedside table.   Jean then produced the ready folded flannel, cool and damp, from the pocket of her apron and swiftly placed it on Fiona's forehead giving her instant relief.

'How are you feeling now dear? You do look a little pale.   I came in earlier this morning when I got up. It must have been about six o'clock and I heard you calling out in your sleep. You sounded quite delirious saying all sorts of strange things; "the walls are alive" you kept saying or at least that's what it sounded like anyway.   I can't quite remember your exact words, you were a bit incoherent most of the time, but you were so hot, I thought you had a fever, and so I opened the window and cooled you down with a flannel until you quietened and then eventually you went back to sleep.'

Fiona responded apologetically, 'I'm so sorry mum I hope I didn't make too much noise.'

'Well, you woke up poor Alf you know. I found him wandering around outside your room looking very upset and agitated but I sent him back to his room and told him I would look after you.'

Fiona sat up suddenly, remembering what had happened,
'Yes, yes of course, I remember Mum, Alf was there, he was there in the tunnel.'
'What tunnel?' queried her mother feeling Fiona's forehead again and gently pushing her back down to the soft pillow.

Jean busied herself tucking Fiona into her sheets and blankets wrapping them round her tightly concerned that she still appeared to be a little delirious.

Jean stopped at the door on her way out with her hand on the handle,

'Now listen, no more talking nonsense, I want you to stay in bed for the rest of the day and rest. Make sure you drink your tea and I'll bring you a small piece of toast later.'

Jean closed the door behind her and the latch clattered into place as she left the room and headed for the stairs.

Fiona lay for a while, thinking over the events of the night before. She shivered as she remembered how scared she had been but she really did feel ill? Perhaps in her feverish state she had imagined all of it. She really must get some kind of grip on reality! As she lay with her head back against the pillow she looked down towards the end of the bed and saw her beautiful blue robe had a murky stain on it. As she reached down to examine it more closely, her senses reeled at the strangely familiar musty smell which convinced her that some of it, at least, had been all too real.

Chapter Nine:

Alf remained in his room as long as he could the next day. He paced up and down and thought long and hard about the events during the night.   He had a problem, of that he was sure, but what should he do about it? He hoped and prayed the girl would not remember much of what had happened during the night. Perhaps she could be persuaded that it was just a bad dream?

As he gazed out of his small turret window his eyes were drawn across the rooftops to the spire, the highest point of the cathedral, just visible as it soared into the clouds. Was it a sign, he thought? Perhaps he should go and talk to Reverend Jeffery. Maybe this time he would help him? In all honesty he didn't hold out a lot of hope but he felt he had no other choice and so without pondering the problem any longer he grabbed his old grey overcoat, a cast-off from George, from the hook on the back of his door, and headed downstairs and out towards the Abbey.

As he entered through the cedar door and stepped into the Abbey's cold interior he stopped and drew in a steadying breath.   He always enjoyed the feeling of peace and tranquillity that emanated from within. He closed the weighty door behind him and stood reverently for a moment or two and then hurriedly made his way along the wide stone corridor to the end of the nave. He knocked on the familiar oak panelled office door and waited for the usual lengthy pause. On hearing the word 'Enter', always uttered in the same slow monotone voice, he turned the solid brass handle and quietly slid through the opening shutting the door firmly behind him.

He stood for a while looking down at the top of the rapidly balding head of Reverend Jeffrey.

For a man of the cloth Jeffrey Pitt was rather self-absorbed with little time for others and their problems. He enjoyed the trappings of being a clergyman, the comforts of wealth and his status in the community but most of all he loved the awe and adoration he received from the congregation. He managed to conceal his inadequacy quite well however with a talent for smoothing things over with a pretension to care. He received gratitude and praise from others wherever he went and considered his place in heaven was assured.

Eventually with great condescension he decided to look up at his caller, blanching almost immediately, at Alf's worried expression.   Jeffery's heart began to sink as soon as he recognised his visitor, recalling Alf's previous ramblings on other occasions over the years; however he cleverly disguised his antipathy as he rose slowly and politely bade Alf to sit down at the table in front of him.

'What seems to be the problem, Alf' he said, closing the book of Accounts he had been working on.   The ostentatious leather chesterfield he'd desired for his office would just have to wait. He leaned back in his chair to study his guest. He had hoped he'd seen the last of this troublesome chap with his strange ideas.

Alf hesitated. He had never been quite sure whether any of the stories he'd told Reverend Jeffrey in the past had ever truly been believed by him but he had no one else to confide in and it was true that he always found comfort in these surroundings and felt a great sense of relief after every visit. He decided to continue.

'I am afraid there is a disturbing possibility that someone else knows about the tunnel in the cellar, Reverend. Her name is Fiona and she is a member of the family who run The Pilgrims Rest. She followed me down there last night. I'm not sure what she witnessed but when I found her she was unconscious. Luckily I managed to carry her back to her bed without being seen. This morning I overheard her mother saying she was suffering from a fever and had been delirious through the night and so there is a chance and I am praying a good chance that she may think the whole thing was a dream or a nightmare. What do you think Reverend? Should I tell her of the tunnel's true significance, to warn her of its danger? I came to you for advice, what do you think I should do?'

Reverend Jeffrey sat forward in his chair and rubbed his forehead as if in deep thought whilst trying to mask his distaste for this familiar subject of conversation. He pushed back his chair and walked slowly towards the window overlooking the Abbey Orchard. He stood for a while gazing out at the peaceful green haven and drew in a deep breath. He was getting rather tired of Alf and his paranoid ramblings and yet he would keep coming back. What to do, what to do? His eyes rested on the parch marks in the grass which showed where the foundations of the old demolished Abbey buildings had been centuries before.

'Ah yes, the tunnel' he repeated thoughtfully. 'I remember Alfred, when you first visited me and told me your story. I could not believe that such a thing could have happened, but you were so strange then, some of the things you said truly alarmed me and then when we could find no trace of your family, it was as if you had quite literally been dropped here from another time. But whatever happened, Alf, however you managed to arrive here, you need to put all of that behind you now and for good. Why keep visiting the tunnel? You need to build a life for yourself here, try to be happy, get married and have children. You're still young. Don't waste any more time yearning for something that cannot be. It seems you may have aroused this girl's suspicions but you will only make things worse for yourself if you keep going down there. What are you trying to achieve Alf? You really need to stop this.'

'No, no you don't understand, Reverend Father,' groaned Alf, 'I can't stop, I have to go back through the tunnel.   It is true for a while I was content to stay here but I have always felt trapped with no other place to go and more recently I have felt a stronger yearning to go back.   There is a restlessness building up inside of me and now I know there is something I need to do and I have to go back to help put things right. You see, there is something I forgot to do before I left.   I think I was glad to escape that responsibility for a while but now I know I need to go back.   I know there is something of great worth somewhere within the tunnel and I need to understand what it is. I need to protect it and guard it with my life. I do not know its true significance but I believe all will become clear to me in time.'

Reverend Jeffery stood quietly digesting this new information and finally with a little more zeal he returned to his seat and leaned forwards inquisitively,

'Hmm, something of great worth, you say?'

Jeffery discovered that he was becoming much more interested in what Alf was saying;

'But why can't you go back? What appears to be the problem?' he queried.

Alf frowned dejectedly, 'Unfortunately there appears to be a problem within the tunnel.   I seem to be able to only get so far and then there is some kind of blockage which I cannot get past. I feel sure if I could get beyond that place, that dead end, I am convinced I would be able to return. Of course I have considered the possibility that there may be another way of accessing the tunnel perhaps via the tobacconist shop opposite and so have been investigating that option also. The owner seems quite oblivious to the fact that he might have a tunnel under his property but I have managed to persuade him to let me investigate a rat problem. He was doubtful at first but then he agreed and I have managed to explore his underground cellar on a couple of occasions, but so far I have had no luck in finding a possible opening. I may have to dig underneath his cellar but that would be a lot more difficult to conceal. Perhaps you could investigate again from your end Reverend? Did you manage to find out if there is or ever was a tunnel under the old Abbey?'

Jeffery conferred a resigned sigh at this old chestnut being raised once again,
'No, I'm afraid not, but well, maybe I will try to look into it again for you, but I can't promise anything and I beg you, Alfred, for your own sanity, try to forget this foolishness and turn your mind to a more useful and positive life.'

Alf rose wearily, shook hands with Reverend Jeffrey, and thanked him for his time. As he opened the door he turned back and said sadly 'I wish I could forget it all, I really do, but something or someone is beckoning me, taunting me almost, and I haven't the will to fight it anymore.'

With a final heavy sigh he closed the office door behind him and strode purposefully along the nave and out towards the tobacconists shop once more.

Reverend Jeffrey sat for a while mulling over what had just passed. He had known Alf for many years now, a tortured soul searching for someone or something, perhaps a key to a hidden door in his past. He had put it all down to a little eccentricity which he liked to believe was a facet of many a sane person's character, but now he was a little unsure. Alf was becoming obsessed with this idea that he had come from another time and Jeffrey began to feel that perhaps he was a little out of his depth in dealing with this matter. Oh how very tiresome he thought; he would have to speak to the Dean or the Archdeacon for advice about this, should he do it now or wait for the next Parochial Church Council Meeting? Reluctantly he picked up the phone.

Chapter Ten:

Fiona had started to feel much better, the small piece of toast she'd eaten had definitely settled her stomach and her head felt clearer, but her mother was insistent that she rested in her room for a while longer. She leant lazily against the bedroom window sill gazing outside and watching the heavy traffic as it trundled its way to the top of Holywell Hill. She listened to the idling engines of the cars and buses and the hissing grating sound as the brakes ground to a halt when the traffic lights turned red. She enjoyed studying the pedestrians as they rushed about carrying their bags of shopping and darting across the street if the road became clear.

Suddenly out of nowhere she spied Alf in the middle of the road weaving his way through the stationary traffic and heading south towards Sumpter Yard. It looked as though he was making his way towards the Abbey?

Without a second thought her decision to follow him was made. She grabbed her coat, slipped on her shoes, ran down two flights of stairs and was out through the shop doorway in a matter of seconds. She must be careful though, she thought, stopping as she got to the edge of the road, her pulse racing. She did not want him to know that she was following him and once across the road she walked quickly but as inconspicuously as she could. A few moments later she caught sight of him just ahead of her under the cedar tree. She quickly hid amongst a group of school children who were milling around the tree making scribbled notes on their clipboards during a day trip to the Abbey.

She watched him disappear into the visitor side entrance and after a few moments, decided to follow him. She turned the solid brass handle of the cedar tree door and pushed it gently inwards.   It was a thick, hefty door and she allowed just enough of a gap to slip through without being noticed. As she entered the quiet interior, she quickly looked around. She could see only a few visitors inside as it was still quite early in the day but the sound of echoed footsteps and hushed voices broke the silence.   She took in the familiar smell of the Abbey, of its history and otherworldliness, and enjoyed the feeling of serenity. As she surveyed the long nave, in the distance she caught sight of Alf disappearing through one of the heavy oak doors marked 'Private.'

She made her way purposefully across the corridor and stood for a while amidst a group of visitors as she considered what to do next. She really needed to know what was going on behind that door. As she looked further along the corridor she could see another similar oak door not too far away from the first which didn't say private and perhaps if she went into that room she could find out who Alf was visiting. Her plan set, she moved quickly. On reaching the door she pulled down cautiously on the ornate brass handle and discovered the room was unlocked. With no time to reflect whether or not this was a good idea she quickly entered the room and immediately exhaled a significant sigh of relief when she found it was empty. She stood quietly just inside the closed door for a moment and detected muffled voices coming from the other side of the wall.

She moved closer and placed her ear against the dark wood panelling similar to that covering some of the walls at The Pilgrims Rest. She recognised Alf's voice and could hear the sombre muffled tones of another man but could not hear distinctly what either of them was saying. She picked up a few odd words here and there and it seemed as though Alf was asking this man for help, she heard him mention the tunnel and the tobacconist having a problem with rats! She could not make any sense of it but she could hear anguish in Alf's voice and a dreadful despondency. His voice dipped in a melancholy manner becoming almost distraught and then it was raised again almost in anger as finally she heard the door open and realised he was leaving. Before he left she heard him say something about being beckoned and that he was not able to fight it anymore and then nothing but the sound of his footsteps echoing away from her down the passageway. But what was it, what could it be that he was struggling with?

She sat down on the solitary cold leather chair she'd found in the room and drank in the silence. After a few moments she heard the voice again from next door. Whoever Alf had been talking to was now on the telephone and as she listened she realised he was discussing Alf with someone.

Alf returned to the Pilgrims Rest with a heavy heart and discreetly made his way back to his room. He sat, slumped on his bed, his head in his hands. He'd called in at the tobacconists on the way back from the Abbey but the shopkeeper had been so busy with customers that he'd shooed Alf away and told him to come back later.

Alf slowly took off his worn leather shoes carefully placing them side by side and lay back on his small single bed. He stretched out his tall slim frame trying to calm himself as he drew in deep shuddering breaths. He needed to be quiet and still for a few minutes and return to the calm inner peace he'd mastered so well over the years. He had convinced himself this was the only way to maintain a little sanity in his life. But as he lay there he could no longer ignore the seeping wetness as it drained from his eyes and into his soft pillow. He squeezed them shut for a moment, wiping away the dampness with his shirt sleeves. As he cleared his throat he opened them once more and stared ahead at the heavy wooden cross nailed to the wall opposite always hidden from view behind the door.

As his mind wandered, he began to reminisce about events from long ago, from another time, another place. He tried to stop the thoughts coming but it was futile. He knew that inevitably they would overpower him and he would succumb and so he gave up his fight knowing that he would yet again experience the dreadful pain that he could not stop. He had been hardly more than a boy as he remembered all those years ago the reason why he had entered the tunnel.

As a young boy he had been happy and fun loving, free from fear, apart from the odd occasion when his father's strap was applied to his rear end in order to curtail any impudence.

Alf was the eldest child of four siblings with two younger brothers and a smaller sister named Anabelle. His mother had told him that Anabelle had come into the world before she had been properly cooked and consequently she ran with a slight limp. Nevertheless she was a happy intelligent girl who could keep up with her older brothers perfectly well, even fussing over them like a little mother.

Alf adored Anabelle and she adored him in return. While his brothers were off together fighting or playing rough games, he would prefer to play 'tag' with his sister, always letting her catch up to him, aware she could not run as fast as him and then delighting in her squeals of pleasure as she pulled him down by his shirt tails, and they would tumble over and over together on the soft grass laughing joyfully in each other's arms. He would then carry her home on his back if she grew too weary and made sure he was always around to protect her from the bullies and the jibes.

When Alf was about 12 years old his mother had sent him off to the next village to earn a little bit of extra money. He was to help Adam the Blacksmith and also make enquiries about becoming his apprentice and learning the trade. The arrangement was that he would stay the night as it was a fair distance and then return home the following day.

That night Anabelle had not been able to sleep and had woken up coming downstairs in her nightdress. The fire was still alight in the grate and she delighted in the chance to dance around in the kitchen without her mother scolding her. Round and round she danced and laughed whilst the rest of the family were up on the first floor of the cottage fast asleep. The fire fizzed and crackled as her nightdress swirled about her but the ragged hem which hung down swept against a glowing ember catching alight. She ran in panic from room to room as the flames engulfed her, trying to escape the fire, but in each room the dry straw which littered the floor was ready to catch and burn like dry tinder until the whole house was ablaze and the family sleeping upstairs had all perished.

Alf returned home the next day to the sight of a burned out shell. No one could quieten him; his weeping and wailing could be heard across the fields almost half a mile away. He was inconsolable, unable to accept what had happened. In such a short space of time he had become an orphan and for many days he drifted aimlessly in a vast void of emptiness. The feeling of loss overwhelmed him and despair was his constant companion. He felt completely alone and for many weeks he was sleeping in haystacks and foraging for food.

The villagers tried to offer him sympathy and support but he would not hear them. He wanted his family and no one else. Pulling away from their comforting arms and pitying eyes, he ran into the fields and woods to sob. He remembered his mother had mentioned to him once she had a sister who lived in the north but he had no idea how to get there or where she was and so in the end, hungry and tired, he sought refuge at the monastery.

The monks who opened the grand gate to his feeble knocking were kind and merciful, graciously taking him into their care. They fed him and clothed him giving balm to his spiritual wounds and after a few months the aching wretchedness inside began to ease. For the following three years Alf lived within the monastery as a novice monk, learning the art of prayer and forgiveness, finding solace in the serene and structured existence surrounding him within the monastery walls. In this new world of devotion and hope the sadness he'd known for so long began to dim.

His life however was about to be turned upside down yet again when one frosty morning a horseman arrived from London.   The lathered horse paced up and down in the courtyard snorting loudly after the long ride. His mount was a fellow disguised head to foot in black clothing who shouted out to the onlookers warning them that a great change was coming and that the monks and their way of life would not be able to continue for much longer. He relayed the news that King Henry VIII had begun a reformation process making himself Head of the Church in England. A new Reformation Parliament was to be set up and the dissolution of the monasteries was about to begin.

It seemed Thomas Cromwell, Henry's new adviser, had previously visited St Albans during the year of 1536 and reports had been sent back to London of disreputable goings on at the monastery, none of which were true, but the order had come back that all possessions should now be seized and returned to the Crown.

One of Alf's duties at the monastery was to clean and care for the artefacts and Shrine of St Alban. When news arrived of the King's plan the Abbot decided that all artefacts must be taken away to a safer place or buried somewhere in the grounds away from the main shrine just in case. Alf had dutifully removed the sacred sword which had been used to behead Albanus during the third century AD and said to hold miraculous merits. He'd clandestinely taken it from the shrine, wrapping it carefully in heavy sacking, and carried it to the orchard, where he'd buried it guardedly.

A few days later chaos had ensued within the monastery walls as a small army of strong-minded soldiers had arrived and meticulously searched every room seizing anything that might be of value. Every item of gold, silver, bronze or lead was taken away to be melted down. The few remaining monks and nuns found cowering in their monastic cells were herded outside like sheep. Fearing for their lives they quickly fled to other religious houses for refuge allowing the soldiers to continue their pillage.

William, one of the elders, had mentored Alf over the years and urged Alf to flee to safety.
'Go to the tunnel' he'd advised him, 'head for the cellar, you'll be safe there for a while at least.'
'What about you William? Where will you go?' Alf pleaded, not wanting to leave his friend.
'You're a good lad Alfred, but you don't need to worry about me, I'll be fine. I know many hiding places. I will call upon our dear Lord for safe deliverance from these evil doings and I pray fervently that we will see each other again very soon. God speed to you my dear boy.'

Alf then fled into the same tunnel he had used many times before when accompanying William on their regular winemaking trips. He knew the tunnel well and that it travelled deep underneath Holywell Hill ending at the cold dark cellar on the other side where the monks kept their wine stocks. Pilgrims journeyed long distances to visit the shrine of Saint Alban and Verulamium and during their visit they stayed at the inn above the cellar. The monks would give them succour, a bed to sleep on, bread, cheese and wine during their visit. The inn was known then as 'The Pilgrims Lodge.'

Alf recalled feeling a little disorientated as he had stumbled through the darkness. The tunnel seemed to deviate from its normal route and the direction it took was unfamiliar. He was confused at the time but continued striding forwards as fast as he could through the underground passageway. He kept his head down with his arms outstretched, feeling the way with his hands, and surfing the tunnel walls as he went.   The journey through the tunnel seemed interminable and he was mystified as to why this should be but confident he would arrive at his destination soon and to safety.

At last when he arrived at the end of the tunnel, strangely, he saw an opening in the wall he did not recognise. He peered in through the gap and looked around in complete amazement at the transformation before him. The contents of the wine cellar he knew, the stored racks housing row upon row of wine bottles had all gone, and in their place were many other strange objects; packages piled high to the ceiling, other metal items, hard and round, which he now knew were cans of fruit and vegetables, but at the time these were sights he had never seen in his life before. He'd climbed gingerly across the boxes and tins of food and slowly ascended the wooden steps leading up to the cellar door finally arriving inside The Pilgrims Rest.

The hustle and bustle of the unfamiliar environment frightened him and he quickly escaped along the side corridor and out through the door to the garden outside. At this point, he stood at the gate pausing for breath, and he recognised the familiar view through the archway to Holywell Hill. He felt overcome with momentary relief at the sight but his sanity was short lived, replaced with utter disbelief, as the true horror of his predicament materialised in front of him.

There, at the far end of the archway he watched in awe as a queue of monstrous vehicles, noisy, strange and completely alien to him, chugged slowly up the hill.

At the sight of this supposed apparition he sank down on his haunches, horrified, not daring to move, and remained crouched under the archway in abject fear and shock.

Finally, submissively he slumped backwards against the wall, in the damp and dirt, wrapping his arms around his knees and quietly sobbed for what seemed like an eternity, until Nana Win had found him and taken him in.

Chapter Eleven:

On her return from the Abbey Fiona immediately sought refuge in her room. She sat down on the bed, feeling worried and confused about Alf.   The door to his room was closed as she'd walked by and she'd resisted the urge to knock but she was certain he was in there. Her mother had told her she should not come into the kitchen today but stay and rest in her room.   She hoped she had not been seen dashing out and across the high street but she felt sure that everyone was probably busy in the kitchen with lunches and so she doubted anyone had missed her.

She picked up the second piece of cold toast her mother had brought her earlier and tried to eat it but quickly put it down again realising she was shaking a little. She lay on the bed and covered herself with the blanket as she gazed up at the uneven ceiling trying to gather her thoughts. She closed her eyes and tried to sleep but vivid memories of the tunnel walls writhing and moaning caused her to break out in a cold sweat and after a while, she rose again and ventured out along the soft carpeted corridor and across the landing.   Holding on tightly to the spindly stair rail she moved slowly down the narrow stairs until she reached the first floor.   She still felt a little wobbly as she crossed the landing and walked into the dark, gloomy corridor.

She walked past the old sitting room now standing empty since they had moved into the flat, remembering how she used to kneel on the window seat as a child, peering out at the traffic as it came to a standstill at the top of the hill always hoping a bus or lorry driver would look up at her so she could wave back to them but they never did. Strangely it wasn't a noisy room; as it ought to be with the traffic rumbling along outside, but after a while the constant hum would dissolve into the background and the family room would assimilate a warm cosy environment. A memory stirred of Helen and Danny as babies and she could almost visualise them playing together in the little white wooden play pen, a large clothes horse nearby constantly covered in baby garments as they dried in front of the small electric fire.

The next room along was her Grandparents bedroom, thickly carpeted in midnight blue, and with French chateau- white furniture arranged around a large sumptuous bed, a luxurious silken eiderdown neatly placed on top. As a child she would sit at Nana Win's dressing table, well lit from two sash windows either side of it, and imagine herself a fine young lady investigating the wonderful array of expensive perfume bottles in a row in front of her and tidying her hair with the antique silver brush and comb set.

A wad of pound notes, rolled and fixed in the middle with an elastic band, would invariably sit just in front of the large three-piece vanity mirror. The room was never locked and any outsider venturing upstairs would be able to swipe this easily if they were daring enough. A further hoard of tightly wrapped circular bundles, of different denominations, could be found hidden inside the unlocked wardrobe in an untidy pile on the top shelf.

Fiona would often be asked to pop upstairs to fetch some money, normally required for stocking up the till if it was running low and she found that old money, kept in a wad like that, had a strange smell, not repugnant to her, and in fact she quite enjoyed the aroma and feel of so much money.

Further along, into the gloom, a large cupboard was set into an alcove. Behind its double doors was housed a treasure trove of possessions all squeezed into every spare space, corner and crevice inside. The cupboard was so full that when opening the door an item would immediately fall out of it and would have to be unceremoniously shoved back in.   It was almost as though, following their move from Dartford, all the extra 'stuff' that no one could be bothered to go through, had just been piled and pushed into that one cupboard.

Fiona rummaged through it many times finding all sorts of forgotten treasure; a collection of old '78 records had been one such find but unfortunately some of these had been broken and handfuls of small shards of black glasslike fragments were quite dangerously scattered on the floor of the cupboard.   The undamaged records she had found were contained safely within their faded paper envelopes, now edged yellow-brown with age but her favourite was 'Deadwood stage' from Calamity Jane, with 'Secret Love' on the B side.

She would take it to an old gramophone secreted in her Grandfather's bureau only discovered on lifting up the wooden lid and raising it from its hiding place.   She had been given permission to use it and so she would often sit quietly by herself playing it over and over again to her heart's content. She would slide the black shiny record from its paper cover and carefully place it on to the turntable before switching it on. Round and round it would go in a strange bumpy fashion. Carefully turning the dial from 33 rpm to 78 rpm she would gingerly release the catch from the arm of the needle.   The tricky bit was dropping the needle ever so gently down so that it was right near the edge of the record, not too close so that it fell off but not too far in so that the music started too soon but in no man's land so that just the hint of a hiss could be heard before the distinctive voice of Doris Day enveloped the room.

Moving on past the cupboard Fiona avoided the next room which was her Aunt Evelyn's room. George's sister, Evelyn had come to visit the family the previous year and had been invited to stay for a while.   When she'd arrived at the restaurant she was vivacious, bright and bubbly, although a little overbearing and critical.   On observing the family eating their fish and chips one time in the flat she had scolded Helen quite severely;

'No, no, no my dear, you are using far too much vinegar! Vinegar dries the blood you know!' she'd said loudly and authoritatively. Thereafter Helen was constantly checking her veins to ensure her blood was still there.

Evelyn also had an obsession with Spain, talking constantly about it at any opportunity and of her many holidays there and she would sing at the top of her voice in a completely random fashion;

'Oh this year I'm off to sunny Span, Y Viva Espana' and then she'd proceed to link arms with whoever was available dancing delightedly round the room in high spirits and as time went on the family became fonder of her and her odd ways.

Sadly though, a few months after her arrival Evelyn became extremely ill quickly deteriorating into a miserable manifestation of that once lively personality. She became so weak she couldn't leave her bed and sometimes Fiona would go and sit with her in an effort to cheer her up but the task became increasingly difficult and distressing. She saw her Aunt's puny arm held no flesh when she lifted it up off the bed to show Fiona her new dangling bracelet and that her hair was lank and lacklustre as it stuck to her head on beads of sweat. For much of the time her Aunt would lie back on her pillow and stare vacantly into the corner of the room almost as though she were looking at something or someone and all the while tears softly glistened on her sunken cheeks.

Fiona debated whether she should visit her Aunt today, perhaps she could mention Alf and the tunnel in the cellar, but she decided against it. She wouldn't want to upset her Aunt who had probably never been in the cellar.

At the far end of the corridor a room containing a toilet and a small wash basin could be found. The toilet itself was perched on a raised level, almost throne like, with an old fashioned cistern and chain high above it and the black and white diamond patterned linoleum which surrounded it on all sides gave the room an almost Alice in Wonderland quality. A small mirror hung haphazardly by a long metal chain above the old sink in the corner. Fiona had felt very ill in that room once when she had been quite small and remembered calling out for her mother; again and again she'd called but no one came because it was too far away for anyone to hear.

To the left of the bathroom around the corner was a giant carved oak door about 7 feet high with a small golden knob which always wobbled precariously when turned but then suddenly and easily the door would swing open to reveal the most amazing and wondrous room.

Fiona had never seen any other room with a ceiling as lofty as the 'big room.' The proportions of the room were vast and it had always been called the big room for as long as Fiona could remember. In the middle of the ceiling hung a large carved wooden chandelier, with imitation candle like bulbs at the end of each crossed arm, and a drop from the ceiling of around seven feet. It still swung high above the heads of anyone in the room and its grandeur ensured it would sit quite comfortably within the walls of any medieval castle.

Sitting proud against the right wall was an immense dining table of dark mahogany. It was oval in shape, and measured about six feet wide and eight feet long and so highly polished that reflected imagery could be seen in its mirror-like surface. Its matching chairs, four diners and two carvers, were imposing enough on their own with deep-cushioned silk seats of an opulent design in burgundy and yellow stripes. Lastly, sitting snugly in the corner behind the door, was a large matching welsh dresser. Every piece of corresponding furniture was delicately carved with an intricate Indian design.

Fiona considered the table magnificent; although she had never seen it set for dinner, and often wondered why her grandparents had purchased such elaborate furniture seemingly just for show or to fill up the space. Generally if they didn't eat downstairs in the kitchen George and Win would eat from a tray on their laps whilst watching TV. The Welsh Dresser too seemed defunct, devoid of any ornaments, apart from Dougie's Victor Ludorum Cup, won for Sport at the infamous Goring Hall School.

During George and Win's affluent years in the pub trade Dougie had been sent away to boarding school, an expensive 'posh' one in the country. He had been only 9 years old at the time and was used to being with his brothers at the local school, perfectly happy and with no knowledge of such a big change ahead of him which unfortunately turned out to be rather an unhappy one. The younger boys at the school were frightened and lonely, regularly wetting their beds at night, being punished and disgraced for it. Dougie had managed to smuggle in with him a small brown and white panda-like bear kept hidden within his boots and if he was feeling particularly lonely at night, following a day of unrelenting cruelty from the older boys and even the masters, he would nuzzle his small bear for comfort and his furry friend would save him from such embarrassment.

Dougie always laughed when he told her the 'amusing' story of how he'd been forgotten by his parents at the end of term, and how he was left waiting on his own at the end of the drive, until he finally received a message from his parents to confirm that they had forgotten about him.   The school caretaker had delivered the message when he discovered him sitting alone on his suitcase at the school gates, explaining to him that he might as well come back into school as his parents would not be able to drive down for quite some time! Dougie would often exaggerate the story by saying that he'd waited a whole day for them to come and get him and then he'd laugh again as though it didn't matter to him.

Fiona had always known her father to be a positive unaffected individual who always looked on the brighter side of life, but she couldn't help feeling very sad for that poor forgotten boy left sitting on his suitcase alone. Would an event such as this have an effect on his self-esteem she wondered? Was that why he clung to his parents now? Hardly a day went by when he wasn't by their side.

Four crimson velvet wing-backed chairs took centre stage in the big room elevated at their base by clawed animal feet lending a palatial air. Their plain colour contrasted well against the expensive fitted carpet, a richly patterned expanse of small squares covering the room from corner to corner in various hues of blue, gold and red. Each small square contained a repeated design across the floor of royal emblems, Prince of Wales Feathers, crowns, diamonds and flowers which added to the opulent ambience.

The largest of the chairs was positioned near the wall behind the door and belonged to Grandad George, adjacent to this a slightly smaller version for Nana Win. In the evenings when the restaurant was closed, they would sit cosily together watching television. Within easy reach a bulky telephone sat on a small table, tucked just inside the door. There were only two telephones at the restaurant; both were huge and black with unwieldy handsets once lifted from the cradle. The second phone was downstairs on the landing just above the shop and secreted on a shelf-like bureau hidden behind stained glass windows. This was mainly used for table bookings but occasionally Nana Win would covertly use it to place her bets just before the lunchtime rush. Both telephones were ornate and antique looking and after each separate digit was dialled the white and silver dial would rattle noisily back into place.

Two further chairs completed the row of four, empty most of the time, but available for anyone who might want to come upstairs for a rest and a chat, which Fiona often did, always feeling comfortable and safe sitting next to her grandparents in the big room. However very soon she grew to realise that any conversation would always relate to the business and what was going on downstairs, how busy it was in the kitchen, how many customers were in or sometimes about jockeys and trainers and who was running in the next race but very rarely if ever was it about Fiona!

Fiona admired an antique tapestry screen of Madonna and child which was positioned in front of the large open fireplace blocking it from view. The fire had not been lit for several years following an accident which could have proved catastrophic. One chilly afternoon, Sheila, the waitress had noticed a burning smell when clearing the tables downstairs in the long room. She'd gently touched the timbered struts along one side of the room and had been shocked to realise they'd become hot and had started to smoulder. The fire brigade was quickly called and the source of the problem was found to be the fireplace directly above in the big room. The fire was quickly doused and after a few hours the timbers started to cool down and all was well. Safe to say it had never been lit since.

A large modern cupboard on legs was rather out of place next to the old fashioned fireplace but all was revealed when the cupboard doors were opened to reveal a huge television set inside. Not far from it and standing proud against the back wall was a shiny burnished wooden bureau housing Grandad George's gramophone and underneath it a record rack full of his 'Mantovani' LPs. On top of the bureau, in pride of place, sat specially commissioned portrait photographs of the four sons, taken many years before when they were young boys. These were a constant source of scrutiny and amusement to the grandchildren as one of them looking remarkably like Harpo Marx!

Ronnie and Dougie were the two sons who had remained loyal to their parents and helped them take up the reins of the restaurant business and so they were understandably very close. They had a lot in common; the same sense of humour, similar interests in gambling and golf, and a fairly laid back nature - neither of them taking anything very seriously. Horse racing was a regular theme of conversation and if the restaurant was quiet, they would often sneak upstairs together for a quick break to watch a race with George and Win.

Fiona would peer round the door of the big room to see all four of them sitting on the edge of their seats, shouting at the TV screen, willing their chosen filly over the finishing line and then listen to the moans and groans if they didn't win or the cheers and back slapping if they did! This gambling lark seemed a family trait with complete dedication to the study of form relating to jockeys, owners and trainers at the various race meetings. Dougie particularly held a strong belief that one day he would find that winning system which he rely on and his relentless quest for this was an addiction which drove Jean to distraction, with his constant reassurances that she could depend on it, that one day it would happen.

'I know there's a formula, I just have to work it out,' he was for ever informing her, 'I'm so close, I can feel it, I know I will crack it soon.'

Emphatic in this belief, he spent hours poring over piles of old newspapers and form books which cluttered every corner, he wanted it so bad, that longed for success that would make it all worthwhile!

But Win was always the lucky one, regularly making her phone call to the bookies just before the lunchtime races and putting on her well-to-do business voice just in case any of the customers were listening;

'W A Fordham, of The Pilgrims Rest,' she'd pronounce very slowly and distinctly before giving the name of her chosen filly or gelding with a bet of £20 or £10 each way. Of course her horse would always be first past the post or in the first three at the very least, but no one knew how she did it. Was it a hunch or just luck or some kind of female intuition, no one knew, but Win knew that the key to winning was knowing when to stop, to quit when she was ahead; that was the secret of how to win, how to stay ahead of the game!

The Mecca Bingo Hall in Chequer Street was a favourite haunt of hers on a Thursday evening, only a short walk uphill of about two hundred yards, she looked forward to meeting up with several acquaintances she'd made there, and in truth it was the only social life she had. She would regularly return home at least fifty pounds richer, her lucky numbers coming up again and again.

At the farthest wall of the big room four extremely large sash windows overlooked the courtyard garden. Directly below the first in the corner of the garden was an entrance door which led into the lobby behind Anna's room. Here could be found the ladies toilet and the drinks area. Win had insisted many years before when they had first taken on the business that no alcoholic drinks were to be served and she could not be persuaded from this decision, theirs was a lunchtime trade, she said, she'd had her fill of drunkards and revellers during those years in the pub trade. She couldn't forget the stubborn late night loud mouths she'd physically pushed out of the door when they'd refused to leave, always with the knowledge they would return the following night. Let other places in the town deal with that sort of scum.

She had found contentment seeing the friendly faced regulars who flattered her with their praise, families on a pleasant day out wanting to enjoy a nice three course meal; soup of the day or fruit juice, a delicious roast dinner, a mouth watering home-made dessert and a nice cup of tea or coffee, that was all that was on offer here and it seemed that's what people wanted as the place was always full. She was determined there was no need to change.

The kitchen was huge with everything in it you could possibly need; a giant set of ovens, two large tables in the middle of the floor for food preparation, a rickety shelf unit tucked into the right hand corner housing every item of crockery imaginable, all of it mostly matching in a slightly off-white colour, bought as a 'job lot' from the cash and carry store. On a small bureau behind the door sat several trays of cutlery; knives, forks, dessert spoons, soup spoons, tea spoons and even fish knives and forks.   A separate preparation area housed a hot water caddy for filling the stream of never ending teapots, an industrial sized coffee percolator, and a container of hot milk, all were on tap and regularly topped up for the various hot drinks required, including frothy coffee and hot chocolate.

Just at the end of the kitchen and before the scullery a range of industrial gas hobs were always fired up under many large two-handled saucepans, which bubbled and steamed, full to the brim with potatoes and other vegetables of the day. At the back wall a wide squat double fronted fridge was crammed with every food imaginable and just in front of the back door, shelves were full of various commodities, condiments, custard powder, home made melba sauce, treacle and various jams for the desserts. In front of the large seven foot window which overlooked the garden a huge metal steamer perspired and hissed as it cooked the sponge puddings simmering inside on a bed of hot water.

Fiona had often been lured down to the kitchen by the thought of a scrumptious steamed pudding fresh from the steamer. Dougie would grin with pleasure as he lifted up the lid for his daughter, leaning well back from the dangerously hot spout of steam which rushed upwards, and in would go his cloth covered hand as he plucked an upturned metal cup quickly replacing the lid without delay so as not to lose any heat inside.   After carefully removing the protective circle of greaseproof paper from the top of the sticky dough he would tap the cup gently on the side of the table and tip it with a quick shake into her waiting bowl. She would then have the difficult choice of either hot treacle syrup or raspberry jam on top with custard, cream or ice cream - what a dilemma! But once her decision was made she'd have to move out of the way, pretty damned quick, and find a nice quiet place to sit and enjoy it!

Chapter Twelve:

The pretty courtyard garden had been crazy paved and edged with raised flower beds lovingly planted with roses, snapdragons and geraniums. At the far end away from the dining rooms was the entrance to a covered outbuilding where the potato pile and other fresh vegetables were stored. It was a damp, wet area, just outside the scullery window and here Dougie operated the huge potato peeling machine! This large industrial contraption was magnificent in its operation and as he poured the potatoes into the mouth of the machine, lumpy and dirty, straight from the sack, it would whir and wash, rotating the potatoes on the hard surface inside, peeling them in effect, so that they emerged from the chute at the bottom completely white and clean, ready for chipping, boiling or mashing.

As Fiona sat on the window seat in the big room, looking out over the garden, she recalled a strange unpleasant incident. It had been one cold, foggy morning and she had been staring out of the window just as she was now.

Through the mist she thought she'd seen a strange ghostlike figure standing almost motionless in the garden, wearing an old fashioned black cloak and hat. She'd called Caroline over while Helen and Danny were playing with their toys on the floor.

'Look, quick, Caroline, can you see what I can see, under that tree. It looks like a ghost or someone in fancy dress. What do you think?'

Caroline saw him too but was much more matter of fact and down to earth in her outlook and not prone to fantasise like her older sister.

'Oh it's just a customer, silly, probably on his way to the toilet!' she answered dismissing Fiona's supposed apparition and going back to play with the others.

As Fiona continued to scrutinise the visitor in the garden, she watched him move and start to gently kick a round stone with his boot and following this he bent down slowly to pick it up. He stood for a while almost examining the stone he held in the middle of his gloved hand and then he turned around slowly and looked directly up at her at the window almost showing her the pebble he had found. She pulled back quickly out of view, a little scared, her heart pounding.

In that moment of unease she heard a gurgled shriek from behind her in the room.

Almost like a camera taking a snapshot, she absorbed the picture in front of her. Her little brother Danny's face had turned purple in colour and he was gulping like a fish, clawing at his neck, and struggling to breathe. In an instant she realised what had happened!

Earlier on he'd been clutching a small bag of sweets in his fist, laughing gleefully at the gooey gobstopper in his sticky hand which had changed colour, just like magic. He'd squealed in delight each time it happened, quickly stuffing it back into his open mouth to suck some more.

Without hesitation she grasped his ankle in one hand and swiftly turned him upside down. As he hung there, suspended in mid air, she summoned all her strength to hold him still and punched as hard as she could with her fist between his shoulder blades. In that same instant out popped the gobstopper landing in a puddle of puke on the expensive carpet. As Fiona carefully righted him back on to his feet Danny started sobbing, gulping in mouthfuls of air, and she cuddled him to her rubbing his back and smoothing away his tears with her sleeve in almost complete disbelief at the happy ending. The younger sisters looked over at them briefly from the other side of the room but with no real interest while Danny continued to snivel for a bit and then eventually returned to his play as if nothing had happened. He would never know it but by some kind of miracle Fiona, his eldest sister, had just saved his life.

Later on that same day Fiona learned that she was not the only one who had seen the strange looking man in the garden when she overheard her Uncle Ronnie recounting his tale about the 'ghost' he had seen lurking underneath the tree.

His story was that he had been gazing out of the kitchen window that very same morning, and had seen a figure standing in the shadows wearing a strange dark cloak, his face hidden from view under a black, broad brimmed, hat. Ronnie had laughed whilst telling everyone the tale, as if the recollection made it even more ridiculous, and everyone had joined in his laughter when he likened it to a cavalier!

After reminiscing Fiona pulled back the curtains and gazed out once more. Beyond the men's toilet and out through a wooden gate, a row of outbuildings nestled in the yard at the back of the restaurant. Amongst these was housed a car repair workshop. In the distance she could see Graham in his dirty blue overalls, his head bobbing about under the bonnet of a car, as he worked on its engine. If ever the girls were bored, which was quite often, as everyone else was always busy in the kitchen, Fiona and Caroline would sometimes go for a walk through the back gate and wander along past the row of broken down vehicles to the farthest garage to have a chat with the mechanics who worked there. Graham and Peter were friendly enough and often glad of a little distraction. The girls would gingerly enter the male dominated environment with a fascination borne out of innocence as they surreptitiously glanced at the wall to wall covering of posters and newspaper cut outs each one depicting beautiful women with huge breasts on display. Jean had always told the girls not to get in the men's way and not to stay down there too long and become a nuisance but never once had she mentioned the bare ladies on the posters. Fiona found this strange and it became a guilty secret she and her sister shared and giggled about. It was never mentioned to their mother in case she stopped them going outside to visit the workmen.

The girls were also told to keep away from the stray cats which prowled around the outbuildings.

'They've got diseases, don't touch them or go anywhere near them!' Jean had warned them.

Fiona had often pondered the cat colony. She wondered how large the population might be; estimating if she included all the kittens being born recently and they in turn having their own kittens, there could be well over a hundred of them out there. Most of the cats were ugly looking, balding and scruffy, with mangy matted fur as they continually scratched off fleas, scavenging for food, their pus ridden eyes wary and watchful ready to flee or pounce. There was interbreeding within the colony and many of the kittens had birth defects such as missing or deformed limbs. One particularly scrawny three legged cat with a sticky bloated eye had been unsympathetically nicknamed 'Isaiah'! Isaiah would often howl pitifully at the back gate waiting for scraps of food to be offered by sympathetic customers or staff members but this was frowned on by the owners.

Fiona had been walking through the outbuilding once, past the potato pile, when she heard some muffled sounds of squealing. She had gone to investigate but her mother had caught sight of her and quickly called out to her rather agitatedly;

'Fiona, come here will you' she beckoned hastily, 'would you quickly go and fetch me a tin of peaches from the corridor. They're on top of the boxes next to Anna's room.'

'OK,' Fiona answered graciously, and as an after thought she queried, 'mum, I think there might be a kitten trapped under the potatoes, I can hear mewing sounds?'

Her mother told her not to worry and hustled her along successfully distracting her.

Later Fiona came to realise what was going on and had been shocked and saddened to discover the way her parents had started to deal with the cat problem.

Dougie hated having to do it. He'd called in the pest control companies on many occasions over the years trying various means to rid the restaurant of its ever growing cat population, they'd tried gassing them and poisoning them by various methods, all to no avail, as they continued to breed producing more and more deformed offspring until he was left with no alternative but the unenviable task of drowning every new litter of kittens found in a bucket of water outside the scullery at the back of the potato pile.

Through gritted teeth and suppressed emotion her father tried to explain to Fiona the reasons why;

'They're a pest, and they're vermin and a health risk too. Look, I'm sorry love, I don't like it any more than you do but it has to be done. We have no choice.'

'But it's not their fault,' she'd cried, 'to be born and then to die like that in such a horrible way, it's… it's just so cruel,' and she wept at the injustice of it. She couldn't understand how her father could do it, he was so kind generous and loving and this was something she didn't think him capable of. Seeing her confusion Dougie hugged her to him, trying to comfort her, hating to see her so distressed.

'Would you like to keep one of the kittens?' he offered, 'I'll let you choose one out of the next batch ok?'

She looked up at him then, her tears blurring him from view, but she nodded solemnly, thankful at least that she could save one of them from that awful death; a small black ball of fluff with beautiful blue eyes they named Samson, only later discovering that it was a girl!

Chapter Thirteen:

Christmas was a cheerful time at the restaurant, the atmosphere full of anticipation and bon vivant, as aunts, uncles, children and grandchildren all congregated within the restaurant's idle kitchen and dining rooms on Christmas Day afternoon. It was one of only three days in the year when the restaurant was shut; Christmas Day, Boxing Day and Easter Sunday. On every other day of the year it was open and for Fiona and her siblings Christmas Day was a very special time. They would have their mother and father with them all day!

Cousins would gather in the big room before the main event and chat, laugh and play games together and wonder at Nana Win's weird 'dates on sticks' which they would dare to try because they looked a bit like toffee and then spit out in disgust. From about 3 o'clock onwards the Pilgrims Rest family party would commence and every member of staff was invited along with their own family, everyone was welcome!

Anna's room was by far the biggest, holding 20 tables of various sizes, and this would be completely cleared for the party with all manner of food laid out on a row of tables which stretched out along one wall. Traditional party fare such as sausage rolls, cheese straws, sandwiches and trifle would be available but also special treats such as Anna's Sand Cake, a warm circle of golden goodness. When Anna ceremoniously opened the large round tin, holding it open for the children to look inside, the smell alone was enough to send their taste buds tingling, and the pleasure from that moment was almost as gratifying as the first crumbling mouthful. Anna's sand cake was beautiful to behold and made from a secret family recipe from her German homeland, and one which, however much the family members prevailed on her; she emphatically stated she would never share.

Once the eating was over, the party room would be organised with chairs lined up against each wood panelled wall, so that everyone could sit and have a good view of proceedings. In front of the huge Christmas tree, always positioned in the corner of the room by the window, a veritable mountain of presents was piled high. In traditional fashion George would play his role of 'Father Christmas' handing out all the gifts to everyone with no one missed out, from the oldest to the youngest. One year Fiona and her sister Caroline were worried they had been forgotten as they saw the pile was becoming depleted and the present giving appeared almost over when a sudden hush descended upon everyone and Jean called them over to her;

'Look', she whispered, 'Can you see? What has your father got for you?'

Everyone looked over to where she was pointing and suddenly through the curtains Dougie made his grand entrance, carrying a large Magnus keyboard in his hands, its casing made of brown shiny plastic, with four screw-in legs; it even came with a small matching stool.

'Wow! Hooray!' the girls cried out as they both ran forwards throwing themselves at their father, hugging and kissing him with glee as he fell backwards taking them with him and ending up on the floor laughing together. Fiona couldn't wait to get her hands on the wondrous gift, the first musical instrument she had ever owned, well half owned, apart from her school recorder and that didn't count, but she would have to wait until after the party had finished for that delight to come. The feeling of euphoria and excitement she experienced on that day would stay with Fiona throughout many years to come.

Once everyone had opened their presents and an additional second helping of food had been devoured, traditional party games began.

Everyone's favourite game was 'Musical chairs.' 30 chairs were lined up in the middle of the room with Dougie and Ronnie taking it in turns to be in charge of the music on the record player in the corner. The children would laugh and giggle as the girls danced and the boys raced around the chairs until the music stopped, at which point everyone had to find a chair to sit on and quick! Of course each time the music started up again a chair would be removed and so inevitably, brutally even, one person would be left standing, cast adrift, whilst others sat laughing, smug in their own safety. The game often ended in tears for the younger ones – a lesson for life perhaps and at the end of the game with only one chair remaining, the last two people would chase around it, the funniest part of the game for those watching, but the cruellest blow for the participants. Dougie, 'the adjudicator,' would turn away when lifting the needle from the record so there could be no question of any favouritism or cheating going on and the winner would receive a super surprise present, usually a large doll or teddy for the girls and a toy rifle or train set for the boys. At around 6 o'clock when all was done and the party over everyone would go home happy and content!

Fiona thought back over the years of Christmas parties and could only remember seeing Alf once at this social gathering? She'd never really thought of it before but she remembered he had poked his head through the curtains one time to call Nana Win away from the fun for a few minutes but he had not come in to join them and Nana Win had returned to her seat soon afterwards. Fiona felt immediately sad that he must have either been working somewhere or sitting up in his room, listening to all the merriment downstairs but not feeling that he could come and join in. She would mention this to her mother that they should invite him properly next time.

Chapter Fourteen:

In the early years there'd been room for everyone at The Pilgrims Rest. But the two upper floors became full to bursting as more grandchildren arrived and it became increasingly difficult for everyone to be squeezed in. Susan and Ronnie were fortunate enough to be able to buy a house on the outskirts of town in a small housing estate called Batchwood. Jean's envy was evident. She yearned to move out of the restaurant, always wanting a place of her own, her own little nest, but Dougie seemed reluctant to move away from his parents who were getting older now and he didn't feel he could leave them to run the place alone. And anyway, as he explained to Jean; 'We can't afford anything round here at the moment, can we?'

In contrast to Dougie's lack of finances Ronnie was fairly affluent having received a war pension due to his ill health.

Tuberculosis had been the scourge of both World Wars and Ronnie had contracted that highly infectious disease during his conscription to national service in the late forties. For this reason Ronnie and Susan received a much higher income than Jean and Dougie and providentially fastened their feet on to the property ladder a little sooner. But Ronnie had paid a huge price for this so called luck.

The treatment he'd endured at the time had been more than horrific, verging on the barbaric. Major lung surgery had left him with life changing side effects, his breathing seriously affected, and causing him to suffer acutely in the heat and suffocating atmosphere of the kitchen. Fiona observed him on many occasions struggling for breath, particularly in the hot summer months, and found it difficult to comprehend the fervour with which both her Uncle Ronnie and her father continued to smoke 'high tar' cigarettes habitually lighting up together throughout the day.

Jean and Dougie had met in Dartford during the mid fifties. At the time Win, George and the four boys were all living at The Kings Head public house in the middle of Dartford's town centre following their move there from Soham.

Jean had lived all her life in Bexley Heath in a small crowded semi with a pebble dash exterior and she was the seventh born of ten children.   Mabel Mud, Jean's mother, had been callously cut off from the rest of the Mud family because her suitor Bill Hicks had been labelled 'unsuitable' but Mabel had chosen Bill and so the sacrifice was made.   They'd married quickly; setting up home together, with children arriving at a swift pace one after another and from that moment on Mabel imagined a protective shield existed around her family.

She knew how to keep them safe.   She didn't believe in doctors or vaccinations or interference of any kind from well meaning visitors, always using her own remedies to fix ailments, and of course the older children were relied on to look after the younger. Bill brought in just enough money as a bank clerk and they were able to keep their heads above the water line, just.   The family existed in a kind of capsule, a life where outsiders were unwelcome and everything they needed could be found within their own home, games, puzzles, music and laughter.

During the war when the sound of the sirens heralded the start of yet another bombing raid, theirs was not the rush and race to the local Anderson shelter. No! Mabel would call all the children downstairs and the whole family would huddle together in the dark underneath the big wooden dining table.

The doodle bugs would drone on and on above them and they'd all listen in complete silence to the continuous monotonous hum which resonated throughout the house. They knew however that this was a good thing to hear. As long as the murmuring whining sound continued they were safe under that table. It was only when the monstrous machine flying overhead became silent that the fear and dread kicked in and they would hang on to each other tightly waiting for the explosion to come.

Once the bomb had fallen and the fire bells could be heard chiming in the distance then Mabel would tell them;

'That was the school that was!' and they would all look up at her in awe, because she always got it right, she always knew instinctively the exact spot where the shell had landed.

'If we're going to go', she'd say 'we'll all go together.'

Bill, was a quiet contented man, who'd married the woman he loved and was perfectly happy with his lot. They'd never be rich in a monetary sense and to be truthful they were only just able to survive with all of them living on hand-me-downs and scraping together every penny but in other ways their life was full of laughter and fun and the pure enjoyment of simple pleasures was ample compensation. Bill's piano playing was his solace and the family would sit round together and sing while he played. He'd composed a few of his own songs over the years but had never shown them to anyone, they were just tucked in the hidden drawer of his bureau, Bill never feeling confident enough to let anyone else make a judgement on them. Happily he had used his talent to earn a little bit of extra cash as a pianist in his spare time. With ten children to feed and clothe the extra money was very welcome and so in the evenings he played piano at the local pubs.

He had been hired to play piano at The King's Head in Dartford on New Year's Eve 1955 and on that night Dougie happened to be serving behind the bar. Jean had also been invited out on a first date with a chap she'd met at a party the week before.

After waiting at the arranged place for a good twenty minutes or more it slowly dawned on Jean that her new beau wasn't coming. Her pride was a little dented but after another minute or so she realised that she was actually quite relieved. She'd been more than a little tipsy that night and couldn't even remember what he looked like and without waiting any longer she quickly decided to change her plans and seek out her father whom she loved more than anyone. He wasn't far away, she knew he was out in Dartford town tonight and so she'd happily keep him company whilst he played piano at the pub.

As Jean walked in to The King's Head she noticed Dougie who was standing idly at the bar. He looked up at the same time as she entered the room and their eyes locked together for the briefest moment as they exchanged immediate admiring smiles. Dougie's heart managed to do a few crazy somersaults and skipped a beat or two as he watched Jean searching the interior of the pub. He watched her face light up at the sight of Bill, the elderly pianist sitting in the corner and watched with interest as she walked across the pub towards him feeling somewhat relieved.

Jean definitely liked the look of the young man serving at the bar. He had an attractive bashful demeanour and a twinkle in his eyes she found very alluring. She sat down next to her father and quietly explained to him what had happened with her date and he chuckled along with her while she took off her coat. Her father began playing again and while he was busy she decided to go and buy herself a drink at the bar. Dougie was enchanted by the pretty dark haired girl with hazel eyes, she reminded him of one of his favourite actresses, Jean Simmons, and he decided he must make a good impression. He began chatting and found out that she was the daughter of their pianist. Great, he thought, that could mean he might see her again. However as they chatted and he learned that she had been stood up that night he decided to grasp the opportunity to ask her out. That guy's loss is my gain, he thought to himself and so, while Jean was chatting to her father in the interval, Dougie asked Ronnie if he would cover for him at the bar that night. Ronnie was more than happy to help his brother out as he had also started courting Susan the daughter of their brewery supplier, and so the rest, as they say, is history!

Jean and Dougie courted for several months finding they had the same sense of humour, laughing together at the silliest things, and falling more and more in love with every passing day. When Dougie proposed to Jean and she learned that the family would be moving out of Dartford and heading to St Albans she happily accepted. They were to be married in St Albans and she was excited to think about this new adventure. She would be with the man she loved and financially comfortable for the first time in her life.

Up to then her life had been rather hard, being one of ten, she'd spent most of her young life helping her mother with the chores and with the younger siblings. She'd recently managed to get a job as a secretary in London earning a small amount of money to go into the pot but now perhaps she could help more. They'd have one less mouth to feed and perhaps she could send them money from the new business every now and again? She was sure her new husband would allow her to do that. All of her young life, she'd had to scrimp and save with a 'make do and mend' mantra etched into her psyche. She looked forward to the future now, joyfully, with the financial burden lifted from her shoulders.

Little did she know how much hard work and strife lay ahead of her?

Chapter Fifteen:

A group of Fordhams sat in a worried huddle around the large square kitchen table discussing the day's takings;

'We've got to put the prices up,' said Dougie exasperated, 'there's no way round it. We're just not making enough money.'

'No!' said Win forcefully, 'the place is always full, if we start putting our prices up people won't come any more, they'll soon find somewhere cheaper!'

'Mum, don't be so daft, of course they will and we've got to pay the bills, and the wages, not to mention the rent! Cooper's talking about putting it up again next month. Anyway, so what if we lose a few regulars to start with, they'll come back, there's nowhere else in town that can beat us for good value. We've got to do something or we'll start losing money in a minute what with the prices at the cash and carry going up.'

Dougie tried to calm himself! He hated arguments and always walked away from confrontation, turning the other cheek and letting others argue the toss! Anything for a quiet life! But his easy going nature was being sorely tested today and he was determined to stick to his guns; they had all worked so hard to build up the business, seven days a week, every week for nearly twenty years. He couldn't see it all slip away. He racked his brains for a way out;

'Maybe we could reduce the staff; let one of the waitresses go. Vera's on the fiddle and everyone knows it? Perhaps Anna could manage another room. She'd like the tip money.'

'If only we'd bought the place outright when we had the chance' Jean reminisced. We should have gone to the banks and begged or borrowed the money from somewhere', she ranted, 'but now old Cooper's got us just where he wants us, working like crazy and taking all our profits. He doesn't even maintain the place; it's all down to us. We're stupid, that's what we are, stupid!'

'Susan and Ronnie want to pull out,' Dougie complained sadly, 'Ronnie's struggling to cope with his breathing going downhill, he's not a fit man and he needs a break. I think we might have to stop the afternoon teas, you know, just do lunches, may be just for a while, and see how we go? We'll save on the wages and the electricity in the afternoons. What do you think Mum?'

Win sat thoughtfully for a while mulling it over. George started to say something but Nana Win gave him a withering look and he knew well enough to keep his mouth shut. Win knew things had been tight recently but she liked being busy. She wasn't sure she wanted to give up the afternoon teas. She quite liked the quietness of the afternoons after the busy lunchtime and to do nothing in the afternoons seemed a bleak outlook. She looked up at the expectant faces, feeling the pressure.

'Hmm, well I suppose it has been quiet in the afternoons recently but what about Anna and the other girls? They might miss that money and we don't want to lose any staff?'

'I don't think we will,' replied Dougie firmly, 'I've got a feeling they'll all be glad to get home after the lunchtime rush. And to be honest people don't tend to tip in the afternoon when they're just having a cup of tea and a scone.'   There was a murmur of agreement.

'OK, then' Dougie declared, 'that's agreed, we'll stop teas from the beginning of next month.'

'We'd better put up a notice to warn people' suggested Jean helpfully, 'I'll type one up and put it on the shop window,' she said, excited and gleeful at the prospect of a few more hours free time with her family, what joy!

The new regime was put into place and the waitresses all seemed fine with the new arrangements. Anna and the two Sheilas had been with the family a very long time and were obedient, conscientious and loyal, rarely saying no to anything.

The owners could no longer turn a blind eye to Vera's deceit in allowing her family members to sneak in for free meals and so her game was up, and sadly after many years' service, she was asked to leave.

Toni and Marion were part timers, happy just earning a little bit of pin money and both were content with the tips they received from morning and lunch time shifts, and so the business carried on in a stronger financial state and with a little bit of profit now being made.

Evelyn's death came suddenly, was of short duration, and not the long drawn out affair everyone was expecting.

Fiona had been sitting quietly on the window seat in the big room, her favourite spot for whiling the time away, when she'd heard a piercing shriek coming from her Aunt's room.   She got up with a start and hurried to her Aunt's bedroom to find her sprawled on the floor tangled in the bedding and whimpering;

'He told me' she was saying, 'he kept warning me, but I didn't listen.'

Fiona quickly rushed forward and bent down to help her Aunt. 'Oh Auntie, whatever happened?' she asked anxiously as she supported her cautiously.

'I don't know…' sobbed her Aunt, 'I just leant across to try and reach my drink and I shouldn't have done it. He knew it, he warned me and I must have leant too far…. Oh my legs my legs, she cried, they tangled up in the sheets and oh my head hurts' she whimpered touching her forehead. I must have bumped my head on the cupboard!'

Fiona helped her Aunt back into bed. She was light as a feather and so it was an easy task. Once she had settled her back against the pillows Fiona examined the swelling which was appearing just above her brow, looking rather like a small chicken's egg.

'Oh dear, Auntie, I think we might need to get the Doctor to come and have a look at you. I'll go and fetch my mother. You stay right there and rest a minute. I'll be back very soon. Please stay still and don't move,' she warned as she left the room.

Fiona quickly rushed along the dark corridor and flew down the stairs. She dodged the customers at the top of the steps and carefully made her way through Anna's dining room full to the brim of chattering customers all sitting at their tables some already eating and some still waiting for their meals to arrive.

She narrowly missed the totem pole of plates Anna was carrying, ready for delivery.

'What the devil?' Anna called out to her, grappling with a swaying stack of dinners, each plate separated by a circular metal ring to keep it warm.

Every dining room appeared to be crowded with customers and waitresses were rushing to and fro to serve them all and so Fiona had to duck and dive to get through. When she arrived at the kitchen it too was frantic and bustling. Through the steamy atmosphere, she saw her mother, standing in front of the oven, placing vegetables on to a plate.

'Mum, she called out, 'Come quickly, Aunt Evelyn has just fallen out of bed, and she's got this huge bump, can you come and see?'

Jean looked up, anxiously wiping her hands on her apron, and quickly following Fiona out of the kitchen. Holding hands as they went, as if to draw support from each other, they hurriedly reached Aunt Evelyn's room. On entering, they both saw that she was asleep. Immediately realising this could be a bad sign they rushed over to her.

Jean leaned over and held her face with both hands, as she called out frantically;

'Evelyn, Evelyn …. Are you alright? Can you hear me?' There was no answer and so Jean turned quickly to her daughter.

'Fiona, hurry and go downstairs to the telephone and dial 999 for an ambulance, quick ….'

After a great deal of noise and commotion; the sirens, the ambulance men, the frantic looks, and the trepidation evident in the faces of all family members, they stood with comforting arms around shoulders, watching events unfold. Eventually, after what seemed like an eternity but in fact was only an hour, it all quietened down, but everything they'd done was useless and futile. Aunt Evelyn died that afternoon.

At first Fiona felt terribly guilty but she couldn't really understand why? It wasn't her fault that her Aunt had fallen out of bed and died peacefully without any warning. Suddenly it dawned on her, she knew the reason!

Not long after her Aunt had been pronounced dead an overriding feeling of relief had prevailed. This was surely a blessing, she'd thought, a much better way for her aunt to die - quickly without prior knowledge and more importantly without further pain. Evelyn would not have to endure the face of pity on every visitor at her bedside as the final ravages of lung cancer were exposed.

But more importantly Fiona realised that this turn of events was better for her; for she would not have to witness her Aunt's prolonged demise? The mere thought of having to watch her Aunt gradually deteriorate day by day in that room had filled her with dread.

Death and what it meant had filled her thoughts many times. Was it the end of everything?

Fiona had been 6 years old when the concept of death first manifested itself in her thoughts and that those people we love will eventually grow old and die. The fear of this had kept her awake on many occasions. One particular night when the moon was peeping through her bedroom curtains and changing the shape of the dark shadowy corners of the room, her anguish had driven her downstairs in search of her mother. Jean heard her sobs from the sitting room and had come out to meet her at the bottom of the rickety staircase. She'd knelt down on the bottom step trying to comfort her daughter rocking her gently as Fiona cried loudly for the longest time in her mother's arms, begging her not to die.

Chapter Sixteen:

Life went on at the restaurant, the normality of a daily routine soothing jangled nerves and the laughter returned downstairs, although upstairs Aunt Evelyn's bedroom remained empty.

Occasionally Fiona would enter the room and experience its cold tranquillity and an eerie sense of loss. The large four poster bed, in its central position, still dominated the room and the blue carpet was like a sea around it. Fiona thought of her Aunt's decline during her stay, and how she had gone from the vibrant lively woman who had arrived fully made up with a beautifully coiffed chignon bun of blue-grey hair and laughing eyes to the living breathing skeleton that had lain pale and wan on that bed.

Towards the end of her illness her Aunt had begun to hallucinate, informing everyone who visited her that Robert had been to see her again. No-one knew who Robert was but she insisted he was always there in her room. 'He's a very polite, kind man' she'd say. He always takes off his hat and bows to me.'

The image of her aunt lying sprawled against the pillows often replayed in Fiona's mind, haunting her almost and she would quickly shut the door and walk away.

After a few months, when the trauma of Aunt Evelyn's sudden death had begun to fade, Win impulsively decided to take in some lodgers.

'It'll help with the finances' she explained briefly.

So Evelyn's room was no longer empty and, rented out to a man in his late thirties, called Paul. Paul turned out to be a bit of a loner with a sallow nondescript face and rather long, lank, sandy brown hair. He was nice enough though and willing to help out with any chores. The second lodger was called Harry. He was a little older than Paul and occupied the twin room.

The twin room was a rather dark, gloomy room, quite large, with wood panelling on every single wall. It was linked to the big room by an adjoining door. From inside the big room this door was hidden behind some velvet curtains held in place by a gold coloured bronze pole. The door was never opened or at least Fiona had never seen it open. She had always assumed it was called the twin room because it had two large beds in it but later on wondered whether it was due to the two rooms being linked side by side like conjoined twins.

Perhaps hundreds of years ago a high official, or dignitary, or even a member of royalty might have stayed in that room with servants nearby in easy attendance? How exciting that thought would be! And it did seem, whenever she entered the twin room, an atmosphere of nostalgia reigned within. If she stood quietly she could almost hear the hushed whisperings of servants as they tended to that person's every need as he or she lay in the four poster bed.

Win enjoyed her new role as landlady and was up at 6 am every day ensuring the lodgers had a good breakfast before they went off to work. Since the decision was made to stop the afternoon teas she found she had too much time on her hands. She needed to be busy, mind and body, and this suited her well and gave her a new motivation. She still had plenty of energy and strength for one so small even though she was now well into her seventies

Alf kept to his room following all the changes, out of the way of the hustle and bustle. Fiona only caught glimpses of him now and again and whenever he saw her he would quickly dart away.

Susan and Ronnie's house was about 2 miles out of town. It had three bedrooms and a pretty garden with trees and shrubs. Ronnie was happy there. He would sit looking out at his garden or he would put on his boots and potter sometimes, checking on his vegetables and rhubarb. Fiona told everyone that she had never tasted anything as good as Uncle Ronnie's rhubarb and one day he told her his secret;

'It's growing on an old coal pile' he whispered 'that's good black soil that is, and fertile' he said, showing her the damp wet earth and rubbing it between his fingers and thumb. He smiled at her then and winked conspiratorially.

She loved her Uncle Ronnie and he in turn had a soft spot for his brother's eldest child. Ronnie was gentle and quiet, the eldest of the four boys. She knew her father looked up to him and respected him for his wisdom, but was protective of him at the same time. They were true allies, leaning on each other for friendship and support.

Ever since Susan and Ronnie had moved out of the restaurant, Jean had yearned for the same. She'd hinted and cajoled, trying every tactic to persuade Dougie that they should also move out and get their own place.

'It's so crowded here now with all the lodgers' she lamented, 'we're only doing lunches and we don't need to be here all the time. Are you listening, Dougie, stop looking at those racing papers for a minute will you?'

Dougie put down his pen and after rubbing his hands over his face to wipe away the cogitation of jockeys, riders and trainers, he leant back in his chair, looking up at last and tried very hard to listen to what she was saying.

They were seated in the upstairs flat at the small table by the window which overlooked the garden. Jean sat down opposite him.

'Just listen a minute will you? I've heard about a semi in Marshalswick, not far from town' she said, trying very hard to contain her excitement. 'The garden is over a hundred foot long and it's only £5,200. I'm sure we could afford it if we were careful Dougie and then we'd have our own house!   Oh wouldn't that be wonderful?' Jean implored grabbing his hand across the velveteen tablecloth.

Dougie was thoughtful. It might work. If George and Win could start the meat cooking in the morning, he could get to the restaurant for around eight thirty to chop up the vegetables and of course a lot of the preparation for the next day could be done in the afternoons now that the restaurant was closed for teas. He smiled down at her excited eyes, 'Ok, we'll go and have a look at it tomorrow.'

Jean sighed with relief as she ran round to his side of the table and hugged him tight.

Everything happened quickly after that. The house turned out to be just what they wanted and the whole family upped sticks at the beginning of April that year leaving behind their spooky sixteenth century town dwelling for a much more modern 1930s semi in Marshalswick.

A strange freak cold spell occurred just as they were moving into their new home and Fiona awoke on that first frosty morning shivering with cold.   Rubbing her fingertips in a circular motion over the icy frosting covering her bedroom window she peered out at the silent, snow laden world below. Quickly she got dressed and ventured downstairs to look for warmth and company.

She found the rest of the family sitting in front of the coal fire which had been lit in the grate at the far end of the room, a casing of old newspapers stuffed inside it curling and browning at the edges. The new sitting room was cosy and warm but through the French windows she saw that their new hundred foot garden resembled a white landscape and there was at least two feet of snow perched in a heap on top of the privet hedge!

It felt strange living there at first and for a long time Fiona missed her room at the top of the spindly staircase and often wondered about Alf and his strange and lonely existence in the room two doors down from her own but after a short period of adjustment they settled in and her mother's happiness was tangible and infectious. Jean felt free for the first time in her life, free to be her own boss, to make decisions about her family and her life which didn't have to involve anyone else. The restaurant was of course still a large part of their lives. Jean still worked with Dougie at the restaurant every day and of course the children were never far away. The only difference was that they didn't sleep there any more.

One day, a few months after they had moved in, the new, recently installed and very modern cream coloured telephone rang shrilly in the hall. It was late one afternoon and Fiona instinctively knew something was wrong. She heard her parents talking in soft whispered tones in the hallway and not long afterwards they both appeared at the doorway to the sitting room. Fiona looked up and saw her mother sobbing quietly into Dougie's shoulder as he stood awkwardly with his arm around her shoulders looking very solemn. This was the first time Fiona had ever seen her mother cry. Jean never cried. She was always the tough one, the strict one, always able to say 'no' and mean it.

'No, you can't have a snack' she'd say determinedly, 'you will have to wait for dinner!'

Dougie was the soft one, always the yes man, but on this occasion he needed to be strong for Jean.

He stood with a sad, faraway look on his face, not quite sure what it was he should be doing as Jean sniffed into his crisp white handkerchief, spotlessly clean and pressed in pristine fashion by Jean herself, and placed in his drawer ready for his trouser pocket every day. He chanted a memory check and mantra unfailingly every morning before he left for work; 'cigarettes, lighter, handkerchief, money,' patting his pockets as he said it to ensure everything was where it should be.

He cleared his throat and explained to the children in sombre tones that Grandad Hicks had suffered a severe heart attack and he wasn't expected to live. He told them that Jean would have to go away for a while to be with her own mother, Nana Hicks, and all her brothers and sisters.   Fiona listened, hearing his words through a fog of confused emotions, until suddenly she felt very cold and alone. She hugged her siblings to her for their comfort, as well as her own, as the severity of the situation gradually began to sink in and the penny dropped that as the oldest she would be expected to take responsibility for her siblings, she would be taking on her mother's role for the time being.

Jean came downstairs utterly distraught after quickly packing an overnight suitcase. She hugged all her children close, arms wide around all of them, unable to hold back the tears as she said her goodbyes and then Dougie drove her back to Kent, to the womb of her childhood where the family huddled together once more in that pebbledash house where she'd grown up, and then he left her there driving home alone late that night.

Within a few days a further heart attack proved fatal for Bill, who lay dying on a crisp white hospital bed, a former fighter pilot and hero from the first World War and a survivor of the second, a hard working father of ten, he died surrounded by his family aged 73.

Dougie was completely lost while Jean was away; a sailor cast adrift without his compass, a moth without a flame, as he wandered from room to room searching for something, he didn't know what, that thing of importance which was missing, and without it he had no aim or direction. Fiona tried to help him but he was brusque with her and just gave her short sharp instructions like;

'Hurry up and lay the table' or 'go and help get the kids ready for school.'

He would cook them all egg on fried bread with beans every night while Jean was away, apart from one night when they had sausages, which was ironic considering the variety of dishes he served on a daily basis at the restaurant.   One would have thought he'd rustle up something a bit more exciting! But he seemed a different person without Jean. He was just going through the motions, keeping busy until she returned.   No one complained, and even Danny was well behaved, quietly eating what was put in front of him aware of the tense and sombre mood.

Fiona had encountered death for a second time and it frightened and worried her, bringing back thoughts that one day her parents would not be there for her and her siblings, and she suddenly felt alone again as she contemplated the inevitable.   She quickly came to her senses though and realised that for now at least she was lucky. She had a close, warm and loving family around her and then her thoughts turned yet again to Alf and his solitary existence.   Her heart went out to him and she promised herself that she would seek him out on her next visit to the restaurant.

Once the funeral had taken place and Jean had returned home everything gradually settled back into the same routine as before except that there were more frequent visits to Nana Hicks in Kent.   The silver lining for Mabel following Bill's passing was that she was not alone in her grief.   Jean's older unmarried sister, Queenie, continued to live in the house with her mother and they remained the closest of companions, comforting each other with understanding and humour, as side by side they revived the Hicks family tradition of merriment and laughter throughout the many years ahead.

Fiona did harbour a slight suspicion that whenever their visits to Kent took place Mabel and Queenie endured rather than welcomed the magnanimous family of six from Saint Albans as they swooped downwards into the house bestowing gifts on the two women huddled together in their tiny kitchen. The pair would watch with trepidation as one by one the family members descended the stone steps outside, steep and precariously higgledy-piggledy, all the way down to the front door. The last of them to appear was always Dougie, carrying aloft a large tray of food containing a haunch of beef, a leg of lamb, and various tins full of sausage rolls, mince pies and rock cakes. He would grandly enter the unimposing house where his darling Jean had hidden from the war beneath that large dining room table, shielded by faith and love alone.

Chapter Seventeen:

The 341 bus from Marshalswick could take Fiona all the way to St Peter's Street in the town centre, the journey taking around fifteen minutes. If it was a nice day and she was feeling more energetic she would happily walk in to town and reach it in about thirty minutes. St Albans was a busy and thriving market town, with historic landmarks, pubs and shops enticing tourists and visitors into the area. Many came to visit the Abbey and the roman ruins at Verulamium situated in an extremely large natural park with the River Ver flowing through it and a large lake.

As a child she would spend many happy hours at the lake, feeding the ducks, and running down the green grassy banks of the ancient amphitheatre, stomping across the wooden platform at its centre as she performed to the imaginary crowds surrounding her. The solitary sound of clapping and cheering she received from her mother and siblings was music to her ears and afterwards they would all sit on a blanket on the grass and enjoy the picnic fare they'd brought with them from the restaurant, guarding it from the hoards of hungry ducks, geese and swans.

St Peter's Street ran from the top of the town to the Town Hall with a good variety of shops running along it and a popular market every Wednesday and Saturday holding a multitude of stalls. On her journey down towards the Pilgrims Rest she could stop at the Town Hall and choose either the shorter walk to the left or the slightly longer walk to the right. If she had time she would always prefer to walk through the older more interesting area to the right of the Town Hall which contained cobbled streets, quaint shops and an old pub called 'The Boot.' This was a famous watering hole where the King's army had congregated before the first battle of the War of the Roses in 1455 involving the Houses of York and Lancaster; the white rose of York and the red rose of Lancaster heralding the name. Nearby was the Clock Tower, a famous medieval landmark, which had stood at the entrance to French Row since the middle ages, as had the 'Fleur De Lys' opposite, another historic watering hole.

The route she took through the buildings behind the Boot Inn was a favourite of hers, an undiscovered secret access, meandering a little but eventually arriving back at Chequers Street.   She walked along the small spooky alleyway, a narrow egress between two tall buildings, almost like a gorge, her footsteps echoing as she walked, hidden from view, until she reappeared out of this silent surreal world, and back into the hustle and bustle of the busy street and nearly at the end of her journey with the restaurant in sight. Finally she would have to wait at the crossroads of London Road and Holywell Hill for the traffic lights to change.

From this vantage point she could look down the hill and to the place where Saint Alban the first Christian martyr was beheaded in the first century AD. The legend told that a strange thirst had overcome Albanus while he waited to be executed and that a well had miraculously sprung up next to him and so afterwards this site was known as 'Holy Well', and hence the name. She didn't know if any of this was true of course, it all sounded rather macabre, but all she did know was that she was glad she lived in this time and not then.

When the traffic halted and the lights changed, she skipped diagonally across the road towards the Peahen Hotel and continued down the hill a short distance to Number 1 Holywell Hill and her destination, The Pilgrims Rest.

On this particular day she decided she would try to find Alf and just have a talk with him to find out how he was. She hadn't seen him for a while and so much had happened since they had begun their new life in Marshalswick. She had finally given up her job of washing up at the weekend but she would still pop in to see the family and have a free meal now and again especially on a Saturday when she was bored but she had only ever caught glimpses of Alf going about his chores. He never acknowledged her in any way or encouraged her to speak by a smile or gesture; in fact he always seemed to have a constant scowl on his face. As far as she knew he had not mentioned to anyone the events of that strange night in the cellar.

She walked into the kitchen smiling, her cheeks rosy and glowing after her long walk in the cold winter air. Her mother looked up quickly and smiled and waved at her but then continued serving up the plated meals. Eventually she had a minute to speak to her,

'Hello darling' she called out over the clouds of steam, 'the others are upstairs in the flat watching telly', she informed her smiling but at the same time her attention was taken away by Anna coming through with a large tray of dirty crocks.

'Ok', Fiona almost shouted above the din and quickly moved backwards out of the way, 'I suddenly decided to come in after all. I know I said I wasn't going to but I had a nice lie in and I just fancied a walk. It is such a beautiful day mum!'

Just at that moment her father walked into the kitchen through the back door. He had obviously been outside having a quick smoke. He walked quickly over to her and gave her a hug and she breathed in the familiar unmistakable fumes.
'Dad, your face is freezing!!' she laughed pushing him away.
'I know', he grinned, 'and what are you up to then? Have you come in to help or just do a bit of shopping?'

'I don't know really', she paused 'I might just hang around here for a bit. Are Nana and Grandad upstairs?'

'Yes, they're watching the 12.30 at Newmarket.' 'I've got a bet on to win at 20 to 1. It's an outsider called Red Rum, but I reckon he's got a lot of potential, go and watch it with them, if you like. You might bring me luck!'

He started walking back to the fridge, aware of chores needing to be done, calling back over his shoulder 'Let me know if I've won a fortune.'

'How much did you put on?' she called after him.

'50p' he laughed.

She made a face and groaned.

'Oh Dad, what's the point.   We're hardly going to be millionaires on that paltry amount!' she laughed in good humour but afterwards whispered wryly to herself 'but at least we won't go broke either I suppose.'

'Here you go' said her dad, coming back towards her with a £20 note flapping between his fingers.

'Go on, treat yourself.'

She smiled up at him taking the note gratefully and reaching up to give him a kiss on the cheek, aware that she was being completely spoilt and wondering why he was always giving her money? Was it to assuage his guilt or feelings of inadequacy as a father?   There was no doubt he worked continually hard at the restaurant with no days off, and no respite, seven days a week all year round. She supposed other fathers were at home more than he was but he didn't need to worry, he was loved in turn by each of his children who all felt special and important in his eyes.

Dougie was always more than happy to run errands for them or to go out late at night to pick them up after a disco or a party with never a cross word. The beige coloured Daimler Jag was always waiting just outside the venue and was a comforting sight for the girls.

'Was it good? Did you have fun?' he would always ask as they got in to the car and they would both talk together, gabbling away, telling him how good or bad it had been and how many boys had asked them to dance or not!

On one occasion Fiona had been downhearted. She'd sat down opposite him at the table which had been cleared away after the meal, watching and waiting as his lowered head moved swiftly back and forth between his form book and the pile of racing papers. She'd sighed dramatically to get his attention and he'd looked up.

Immediately she had launched into the details of her dilemma,

'They're just not interested in me dad' she'd told him 'I don't know why. I don't think I'll ever find anyone.'

Dougie was a little confused. She was a beautiful, bright girl but he could see her distress and so he looked at her thoughtfully for a while carefully trying to think of a way to lighten her mood.

'Don't you worry about that' he'd smiled 'just you be patient and wait a while. At the moment they're at that silly age when they're just out and about, looking for a one night stand, but give them time and in a little while when they start looking around for a wife, they'll look for you.' She remembered at the time how much better he'd made her feel and she loved him for that.

She pushed the note deep into her jeans pocket,

'Thanks Dad, you know I did see a lovely dress in Chelsea Girl last week. I might pop up there later and try it on.'

As she turned to walk out of the kitchen, she nearly bumped into Anna who was flying along as usual with some dirty plates.

'Oops, sorry Anna!'

'Oooh Fiona, pleeze be more careful!' Anna complained grabbing the plates and cups before they fell from the tray.

Anna looked a bit hot and bothered so Fiona made a quick exit back along the side corridor. She reached the area at the bottom of the stairs only to find a hoard of people queuing to get in. She looked at her watch. Of course she realised, it was the busiest time of the day. She would definitely get out of the way and so she bounded up the stairs and headed for the big room.

All seemed quiet upstairs, apart from the subdued sounds of the TV set coming from the far end of the flat where her brother and sisters were. She walked on past the door to the flat and entered the tunnelled corridor leading to the big room, shrouded in semi-darkness, the carpeted floor seeming even more uneven than usual. This place is so weird she thought to herself, breathing in the atmosphere, and sensing the secrets stored in its shell over many centuries.

She was jolted from her reverie when she heard shuffling footsteps coming towards her from the far end of the corridor. In the middle of the corridor the person she had come here to find stopped dead in front of her and they slowly surveyed each other in the shadows. Fiona's heart started thumping. What was wrong with her? She couldn't speak. It was almost as if she had been struck dumb, not through fear, but by some kind of puzzling premonition. Alf's reaction was furtive but she realised this was her moment, her opportunity to cross that bridge of uncertainty. She had to say something to him.

She finally heard herself whispering in a croaky voice,

'Hello Alf, how are you.'

He stood in silence for a short while until finally he touched his cap, nodding ever so slightly, and answered gruffly,

'Arf'noon Fiona.'

For a while they both gazed at one another, each trying to gauge the other's reaction through the gloom of the corridor.

Finally, it was Alf who found his voice again;

'I heard that you, you'd...... gone away?'

As soon as he spoke the words he immediately wanted to retract them. To his own ears his words sounded forlorn as though he'd felt somehow abandoned or deserted by her. He thought to himself; was that how he felt? He didn't want her to think that. He didn't want her to think he had missed her.

He was right though.... she had heard the loneliness in his voice and suddenly felt terribly to blame for not seeking him out sooner.

'Yes, sorry' she answered in hushed tones, 'we all, just my family I mean, we all moved out a few months ago. It happened so quickly. My mother and father found a house in Marshalswick which is a small housing estate on the outskirts of town. But it's not too far away', she added almost apologetically, 'only about 2 miles. I'm always popping in to town and the restaurant; but I haven't seen you around recently.... not to talk to, I mean.'

'I'm always here' he assured her dolefully then after a short pause added   'I've kept myself busy that's all ... thought it best to keep out of everybody's way.'

She frowned, puzzled as to why he felt like that,

'Is everything ok with you Alf? Is there anything I can do to help you? You seem a little ...... troubled?'

She looked up to see his face but was unable to make out his features and his expression remained hidden from view in the darkness.   However she could tell from his voice and his stooped demeanour that he was truly a defeated shell of a man, lonely and seemingly friendless.

As he looked down at her he slowly and carefully manoeuvred around her. She took a small step back to allow him room to pass and heard him draw in a long breath followed by a sigh before he said;

'If you've got any sense you'll stay away from me. Don't go meddling into things you will never understand. You stay with your family and your nice life.......... and don't go down the cellar any more' he demanded gruffly as he walked purposefully away from her.

 As she stood in confusion, watching him go, she realised how quickly he was walking away from her. He was not shuffling at all.

Chapter Eighteen:

She stood for a while in the dark corridor contemplating what could be done to help Alf. She worried whether it was already too late; his character had become introverted through many years of being alone, perhaps it could never be changed. He found solace in his bible and crosses she surmised.

She shrugged her shoulders and walked on, out of the gloomy corridor, and into the bright cheerful big room. On entering the room she heard her Nana Win shouting at the TV; the race had obviously already started and so Fiona sat quietly at the back of the room on one of the soft silk dining chairs. She leaned back contemplating what Alf had said in the corridor and warning her to stay away from the cellar. Why would he say that? His intention to quell the flame of her interest had seemingly backfired for in her mind the flame of interest had just been rekindled.

She watched until the race was over and Red Rum was unceremoniously pipped at the post, coming in second. Oh dear, there would be no celebration today!

She waited a few minutes watching the aftermath which was mostly a kind of stunned silence and then she moved forwards and sat down next to Nana Win saying,

'Never mind Nan, you can't win 'em all.' Nana Win just grimaced and said,

'You'd better go and tell your dad the bad news. How busy is it downstairs?'

'Quite busy but they're managing OK. Anna seems a bit stressed but I think she enjoys it really. She's got a lot of her regulars in today. Have you and Grandad had lunch? Do you want me to get you something?'

'George, George, wake up George.' Nana Win spoke harshly, and then poked her husband who was dozing sporadically, his head leaning against the wing of the chair. He spluttered and snorted, and then groaned in a cantankerous manner.

'What do you want?' he almost snarled.

'What do you want for your dinner? Nana Win barked back at him, 'Fiona says she'll go down and get us some food. What do you want?'

Grandad sat up cheering up quite dramatically at the thought of a plate of food filling his ample belly.

'Hmmm well now that's a very nice idea isn't it, but what shall I have?' He pondered for a while and then made his decision. 'I think I'll have the Curry and Rice' he said happily. 'It's delicious, even though I do say so myself and I should know shouldn't I, because I made it, ha ha?' he chortled. 'Don't ask me how I do it – just a little bit of this and a little bit of that and the meat, well, y'know it just fell off the bone, tender as you like, mmm beautiful, and a nice hot curry, yes that'll warm me up on this bitter cold day.'

'Okay Grandad,' Fiona laughed at his anticipation, 'curry it is - I just hope there's some left that's all. You know how popular it is! What about you Nana?'

'I'll have the Roast Beef and Yorkshire pudding with just two little potatoes and a little bit of veg please, oh, and lots of gravy. Thank you dear. Oh hang on a minute,' she said thoughtfully as she bent down to retrieve her cream coloured triangle shaped handbag. She plonked it on her lap and released the twisty catch at the top proceeding to rummage around inside for a moment or two.

'Here you go, there's a little treat for you!' she said as she patted a £10 note into Fiona's hand. 'You're a good girl.'

Fiona kissed her Nan on the cheek feeling a bit like she'd earned a tip from the Queen and reflected, financially, she was doing extremely well today!

'Did you want any sauces or salt or anything?' she remembered to ask. It was a long way down again if she forgot anything!

'Just a nice cup of tea for us both, darling, that'll be lovely.' Win turned her attention back to the TV and Fiona took the hint.

'OK, I'll be back soon' she called out to deaf ears as she hurriedly left the big room and turned the corner back into the corridor where she had talked to Alf only a few moments before. She wondered where he had gone after that.

She didn't see him on her journey back to the kitchen. Perhaps he had gone back upstairs to his room. What a strange fellow he was.

As she walked back into the hustle and bustle of the kitchen, she called out her order to her mother.

'You'll have to wait a bit Fiona we're really busy at the moment. Just get a tray ready with knives and forks and you can make their tea while you're waiting.'

And so that's what she did. In hardly any time at all, her mother was sliding the two meals on to the tray she was holding, and as she looked down she marvelled at the sight of the two delicious looking meals and the speed in which they were delivered with a tinge of pride that she was a member of this amazing hard working family.

A few moments later after she'd delivered the dinners to George and Win who were now devouring them with gusto she realised she was a little bored. Her sisters and brother were in the flat watching television and she knew once she went in there she'd never get away and so, feeling a little nostalgic, she made her way up the flimsy staircase to the top floor.

She felt less frightened today of the spooky old attic, after all she was no longer a child, and so she boldly approached the small wooden door. The door was set flush into the wall and was of black shiny wood, similar to that of the cellar door adorned with a black metal ring which she twisted to lift the latch. The door opened outwards to reveal the three wooden steps which led up to the derelict room. Instantly she was struck by the proverbial blast of cold air which reignited her senses as it mingled with the familiar smell of musty cast-off clothing and broken furniture. It was as if she were a small child coming here for the first time many years ago.

Slowly she climbed up the steps and stood quietly for a moment in the stillness. The only sound, apart from the whistling wind, was the creaking from the ancient wooden planks under her feet.

The chilly air blew all around her and goose bumps appeared on her arms and neck. She recognised the same familiar piles of old books and junk still resting in the same place as before covered with even further layers of cobwebs and dust.

She wrapped her arms around her for warmth and remembered a time when she was young and standing there in that very same place. In her mind she could almost hear her silly friends as they ran around out of control in the scary attic, touching things that didn't belong to them, throwing books and kicking at the furniture. Their laughter and bravado had worried her at the time and she was sorry she had brought them upstairs to see this secret place. She'd ushered them out of there hastily with promises of treats from the downstairs kitchen, pulling and pushing them in her desperation to get them out of there and protect the attic from their boldness and lack of respect, almost as though it were a living thing.

'What is it about this place?' she thought as she looked around at the old mirrors, dressing tables and bookshelves crammed with yet more books. She supposed it had all been stored by a previous owner many years before, just unwanted items, left here to rot.

She looked around one last time and shivered a little as the cold draught from the broken window suddenly gusted ruffling the soft frills on her blouse and fanning the tendrils of her fine hair hanging loose about her shoulders. At that moment her eyes became transfixed on something eerily unfamiliar in the long dusty mirror to the side of her. It seemed to resemble some old clothing hanging down over some brown leather boots. As she tried to work out what it could be and where the reflection might be coming from one of the boots in the mirror appeared ever so slightly to shift to one side.

She stared at it frowning in disbelief and confusion. Was her mind playing tricks on her? When she saw it move for a second time a feeling of panic began to crescendo inside her and she hurriedly reversed backwards down the steps. Unhappily her sneakers caught the step at an angle so that she stumbled. She tried twisting round to save herself but instead fell awkwardly careering headlong out of the door and into the open arms of a startled Alf who had just appeared outside of his room.

His strong arms went out instinctively as he caught her to him and they both clung to each other in shock and bewilderment as time seemed to stand still. He looked down into Fiona's vivid blue eyes and understood the uncertainty he saw within those dark liquid pools. Their closeness was intoxicating as ripples of sensation passed between them. As she gazed up into his face, his eyes fixed on hers, she could feel his arms loosen and his hands began to explore and mould her to him. The thrill of holding a woman so close had aroused his senses; senses that had lain dormant for so long. He realised he was enjoying the feel of Fiona's body against his own. Fiona felt it too and was confused at her reaction to him.

Then in a heartbeat reality came crashing in and he put her away from him, straight away putting up his guard.

'What are you doing up here? What were you looking for?' his questions tumbled out accusingly.

'N n nothing really', she stuttered, trying to establish some sort of equilibrium. 'I was just feeling a bit bored that's all. I thought I'd come up here and do a bit of exploring just to see if there were any old books or records up in the attic' she answered him defensively.

'Books?' he queried, 'what sort of books?'

'I don't know, just old books', she went on boldly. 'I like old books! I like the way they feel, the old bindings. I love the smell of them and the history that's in them I suppose.'

She saw his face change from annoyance to one of resignation.

'History,' repeated Alf thoughtfully 'so you like history do you? Well, there's plenty of it to be found here, it's all around us. But you need to be careful what you go looking for Fiona. I'm warning you again, you might find something you didn't bargain for and then there's no turning back!'

'What do you mean Alf? What will I find?' she frowned as she spoke, a little annoyed at his impertinence.

He stared at her for the longest time as if he wanted to say more but thinking better of it he willed himself to stop and just grunted loudly as he turned away from her. Almost as though he dare not trust himself to speak another word he reached out for the latch to his bedroom door and quickly disappeared behind it, closing it vigorously with a loud thud.

Chapter Nineteen:

Fiona stood staring at Alf's door as she tried to make sense of what had just happened. She forgot about what she'd seen in the attic or imagined she'd seen and could only think about the way he'd held her, closer than she'd ever been held by any man, acknowledging then how much she'd been yearning for that kind of intimacy for some time now. Her heart was still racing and her body tingled where his hands had touched and moulded her to him. As she reached up and felt her neck she knew that it was flushed with the excitement.

She found herself wondering whether he had ever been with a woman; she'd had very little experience with men, only a few fumblings with inexperienced lads at parties, but he must be almost forty, nearly as old as her father. What on earth was she thinking? Of course she'd never thought of him in that way, until now. She pondered what he'd said about the history of this place and she supposed he was right. It had been built hundreds of years ago, in the sixteenth century, and yet here they were today, living in it. It was still alive, breathing, holding on to so many stories. What had happened over those years within these walls?

The recent ghostly sightings sent a shiver down her spine and she leant forward slamming the attic door shut. She ensured the latch was tight and secure before walking away from it to the top of the stairs. She looked down again over the rickety banisters imagining who might have lived on the top floor when the building was new in the mid fifteen hundreds. She contemplated that it would probably have been the servants' quarters and the middle floor would have provided the family accommodation. She couldn't imagine the ground floor as anything other than a dining area of sorts and surely the kitchen would have always been a kitchen but who could tell what alterations might have occurred over those five hundred years.

Alf stood quietly listening just inside the door of his room. He knew she was still outside on the landing. He could hear the creaking noises of the old floorboards as she moved around. What on earth had possessed him? He felt he was losing control of the situation.

'Oh Lord' he prayed, lifting up his hands, 'please forgive me please help me to escape this place and this world.' He realised if he was not very careful from now on he might begin to travel an uncharted course, one which was certain to cause harm to himself and anyone close to him.

He walked slowly to the other side of the room and sat down clumsily on the old wicker chair in front of his small dressing table. As the afternoon sun reached out to him through the small lattice window, tendrils of warmth embraced and comforted him as he lowered his head in resignation. He was here, for now at least, and he must make the best of it in this place he called home. He lifted his right hand and placed it over the small ornate bible resting in pride of place in front of him, the only possession he could truly call his own, retrieved from his jerkin pocket the very same night Win had discovered him sobbing under the archway.

Eventually Fiona went downstairs to the middle floor and wandered through to the old flat. The flat was a self-contained apartment previously occupied by Susan and Ronnie when they'd all first arrived at the restaurant in those early years. It consisted of a long sequence of rooms beginning with a large sombre hallway strewn with cardboard boxes containing all sorts of odds and ends and an old piano covered in a dust sheet. Through the door at the end and down a single step a much brighter, more welcoming room could be found with sofas and a large white dresser to the left and windows to the right overlooking the garden. It was a split level room with a small step up in the middle and either side of the step were solid, interlaced, dark wooden beams supporting the original peg tile roof above.

'Hiya you lot', she called from the doorway.

They all jumped up from where they were sitting in front of the TV and ran towards her.

'We're bored!' moaned Danny.
'Yes, me bored too!' Helen agreed, nodding her head vigorously, 'can we go down to the park and go on the ice?'
Caroline stood up and stretched her arms way above her head. She wiggled her body from side to side in a little dance and quickly agreed, 'Yeah, ok, I'm up for it' she said, and then gave a little yawn.

'Oh, alright then', Fiona caved in under the pressure adding, 'even though my legs are still aching from my long walk here! It's alright for you lot, you got a ride here in the car! What about food? Have you all had lunch?'

'Yes', they all shouted together. 'We all had roast dinners and they were fab!' Caroline exclaimed.

'We're full full full to the brim' shouted Danny running around the room whooping and hollering like a banshee 'what about you Fi fi' he collided into her knocking her off her feet so that she fell on to the sofa with him on top of her. She shoved him off in annoyance but his grinning face wiped away any bad feeling.

'Well, no actually I haven't had lunch but I did have a big breakfast before I left home. I had a dad special – egg on fried bread and beans', she laughed, so I am pretty stuffed.'
'Ok', Helen piped up, 'so let's go then!'

Fiona and Caroline proceeded to help the two younger ones get into their coats.

'It's really icy cold out there' warned Fiona as she eased Helen's arms into the sleeves of her brown duffle coat. Caroline helped Danny into his and soon with their hoods up and four large wooden toggle buttons pulled easily through the big loops they finally resembled two small Paddington Bears!

Off they went, jauntily, just stopping off at the kitchen to let their parents know where they were going. Jean fussed and gave warnings to Fiona but finally let them all go.

Hand in hand the siblings sauntered down the slope under the archway and carefully crossed a traffic strewn Holywell Hill. They manoeuvred their way through the queue of waiting cars and entered the safety of Sumpter Yard, a much quieter road, where they could relax a little and admire the view of the Lady Chapel which rose up majestically ahead of them.

Once free of adult constraints they started to run! They ran gleefully along the pavement by the old flint wall speeding past the huge cedar tree and then slowing to a skip along the railings next to the south transept. Finally they reached the top of the park where they turned to follow the grey tarmac path downwards towards the lake. If the weather had been warmer they would have played roly-poly games on the grassy banks but today was icy cold and the ground uncomfortably rock hard so they decided against it and continued walking and skipping all the way down the hill to the very bottom. There they stopped running and waited until they were all together before turning right to walk along the river and past the Fighting Cocks pub.

In the distance just past the bridge they could see the lake.

'Oh look', yelled Helen, 'it's completely frozen over!'

Helen and Danny ran off in the direction of the lake and Fiona and Caroline continued to saunter along behind them, chatting in the cool sunshine about their friends and a new disco which had just started up at the Haven Hotel.

'It's on every Thursday and Sunday' Caroline said excitedly, 'maybe we could go with Louise and Jungle Jane next week?'

'Yes ok', Fiona answered cheerily, 'that might be nice. We'll try and arrange it with them shall we? Poor girl, do you know why she's called Jungle Jane?'

'Hmm, to be honest I'm not really sure, but I think it might be because she has big thighs!' Caroline answered with a big grin and they hugged and giggled together in cruel enjoyment as they ambled happily across the bridge.

As they turned the corner the icy lake stretched out before them. Groups of people and families with pushchairs were bravely tramping across the white wintry landscape and Helen and Danny stood at the water's edge tentatively poking at it with their shoes and scraping patterns in the ice with a couple of sticks they'd found.

'Wait for us' shouted Fiona in mild alarm.

She looked up as a man and a woman danced by, adorned with proper ice skates wearing coordinated turtle neck jumpers, scarves and woolly hats with pom-poms on top. They swirled around together as though in professional competition separating for a while to do a quick circuit and then coming back together again with ease while ducks and geese waddled around nearby perplexed, continually pecking at the hard surface.

'Wow, this is brilliant, but be careful' she told her younger siblings, 'don't go too far ahead.'

They all stepped out precariously and started walking gingerly across the ice towards the strange little island, usually completely beyond their reach, in the middle of the lake. The ice seemed reassuringly deep and as Fiona looked down she could see nothing swimming around underneath it, just solid swirling shapes of grey and white. She crouched down and rubbed at it with her gloved hand wondering if the fish were alright down there underneath all that ice.

She looked up briefly to see that her younger siblings had almost reached the island in the middle and was relieved to think that they would soon be safely off the ice but a split second later she heard a loud crack and watched an impending tragedy unfold in front of her. Her stomach lurched as the ice under Helen's weight began to break up; she heard a sudden splash and watched as her sister floundered, screaming at the top of her voice, her arms flailing as she desperately tried to grab the edge.

Without hesitation Fiona ran, slipping and sliding across the ice, frantically trying to reach the island in as short a time as humanly possible. She'd almost reached it when she saw her sister begin to lose her grip on the muddy bank and slip backwards into the water. As she arrived Fiona reached out instinctively and grabbed the hood of Helen's duffle coat. With all her might she yanked her sister, coughing and spluttering, back up to the surface and pulled and dragged her to safety on the small island's snow-covered grassy bank. They fell on the bank and held each other at which point Helen started to take great shuddering sobs shivering vigorously at the shock of the ice cold water. Danny who'd stood watching it all from his position of safety in the middle of the island found it all incredibly funny as he pointed at Helen guffawing with laughter at the sight of his sopping wet sister,

'You dopey girl', he sniggered.

'Shut up Danny' Fiona berated him, 'we've got to get her back to the restaurant quickly before she dies of hyperthermia,' and then Danny started running around in anguish unhelpfully shouting at them accusingly 'you fools, you fools!'

'I'll help you,' said an unexpected brusque voice from behind them and recognising the voice straight away Fiona turned round. She shaded her eyes with her gloved hand and stared up at Alf's shadowy figure blocking out the sun almost like a halo around his head.

'You?' she replied in confusion and almost accusingly.

'I'll carry her' he said, bending down and scooping her up with ease, showing a strength Fiona never imagined he possessed. Helen was changing colour in front of them, first she was a ghostly white, and then there was a tinge of blue-grey in her pallor. Alf managed to wrap his coat around her legs to keep her as warm as he could holding her against his own body as the group followed behind him walking quickly back across the ice and then along the path and up the hill. He strode out purposefully in front of them, a far cry from the shuffling old man Fiona had known from the past. She could hear Helen whimpering against his chest all the way and Fiona decided, in spite of everything, she was extremely relieved to have him there. She didn't know how they would have managed if he hadn't appeared unexpectedly like that.

Had he been following them she wondered?

It was a long walk back up the hill but Alf marched ahead, the rest of them trailing behind him, and then running in short bursts as they tried to catch up.

'Thank you so much Alf' she garbled, a little out of breath, as they walked. 'I'm so glad you were there to help us'

'No need to thank me, I had to come, I saw him poking and prodding at that frozen puddle with his boot and I knew then, I had to come' he answered flatly.

'Saw him? Saw who? Who did you see?' she queried not knowing what he was talking about.

'The stranger in the garden, the cavalier, he was there out in the garden, and I saw him tap tap tapping away, at the ice.... until it cracked. He knew I was watching him... he was giving me a warning and when I heard them in the kitchen talking about you going to the lake I had to come and find you.' He stopped talking and continued marching up the hill again quicker than before and she couldn't keep up.

She stopped to look around for the others and managed to grab hold of a sharp stick Danny was twirling about his head and throwing it into the hedge as she held on to him, wriggling and whining about his lost sword. Placing his right hand firmly inside her own she endeavoured to pull him away from the hedge and back up the slope. Caroline ran back to help her by grabbing his other hand and they both proceeded to haul him up the hill by distracting him with one of his favourite games; one, two three jump! Fiona didn't get the chance to talk with Alf any further but to be perfectly honest she had absolutely no idea what in the devil he was talking about.

When they finally arrived back at the restaurant, the warmth from the kitchen hit them instantly, turning their faces into bright red beacons within seconds. Lunches were just about over and Jean ran over to them;

'Whatever happened' she asked anxiously, feeling Helen's brow and rubbing her hands and feet.

As the story unravelled their mother comforted them and Fiona gave in to a sudden feeling of emotion and she wept with relief and shock at the enormity of what might have been.

They were so lucky Helen had not gone under the ice, for if she had, she would have been lost to them forever. Someone seemed to have been watching over them that day.

Later on everyone was reprimanded of course; 'How many times have I told you!' scolded Jean. 'You know you can never rely on the thickness of the ice from one place to another. That lake is huge!'

Helen sat comfortably in a small wicker chair warmly wrapped in a large blue blanket. In her pudgy little hands she clutched a milky drink and Jean was satisfied that her pallor was improving, her freckled nose and cheeks were becoming tinged with pink, and she decided the doctor wasn't needed. Alf stood slightly aloof next to the cutlery drawers, ready to escape through the kitchen door, just as Jean turned to wrap her arms around him in an emotionally charged all-enveloping hug which took him by surprise. An emotion surged through him which he kept hidden as he quickly grabbed his falling cap, a memory stirred from long ago and what it was like to be part of a family.

'Thank you so much Alf' Jean almost sobbed. 'It's a genuine miracle! Thank goodness you were there to help them.'

'It's ok, I'm glad to have helped' Alf replied gruffly, shuffling his feet from side to side and looking down to cover his awkwardness while Jean turned away to attend to her baby girl.

Alf touched his cap, adding, 'I'm pleased she's alright.'

He backed away out of the kitchen and its warmth, leaving the family to fuss over Helen as Jean continued to rub her child all over bringing every part of her back to life.

Chapter Twenty:

When all the commotion had died down and they were safe in the knowledge that Helen had suffered no more than a cold soaking and was perfectly well, Fiona couldn't help thinking about what might have been as she cuddled her sister closely to her as they sat watching television on the red comfy sofa in the flat. She wondered how it was that Alf had suddenly appeared out of nowhere and thought about the strange reason he had given as they were walking back up the slope. It was all very odd but she was grateful nonetheless.

She must go and find him to thank him for all he'd done she decided suddenly. Carefully disentangling herself from her sisters' legs she stood up enjoying a long stretch. 'I'm just going downstairs for a bit' she advised her siblings as they huddled together on the sofa engrossed in the latest episode of 'Champion the Wonder Horse'   so much so they hardly noticed her leaving.

Fiona found Jean in the kitchen scooping sugary mince pies out of cooled bun tins and placing them carefully in a large airtight container.

'Mum, do you know where Alf might be. I want to thank him again properly for today.'

'That would be nice darling,' Jean replied momentarily looked up to smile at her daughter. 'I believe he's down in the cellar. He said something about rat poison, so please do be careful.'

Hmm, thought Fiona, that's strange, and she shivered at the prospect of rats running around in the confines of the cellar gnawing away at the boxes and the tins. She recalled the subject of rats being discussed during the muffled conversation overheard on her trip to the Abbey.   Maybe that's what Alf had been talking about, she thought, and why he didn't want her to go anywhere near the cellar! She felt slightly relieved that she'd probably been over thinking things and quickly left her mother to her mince pies making her way to the side corridor next to Anna's room. Dodging the boxes piled up high along the wall on the right hand side, her outstretched fingertips skimmed both uneven walls as she walked jauntily through the narrow passageway. In no time at all she reached the cellar door and pushed it open wide to peer down within.   The familiar dank smell of the cellar reached her nostrils as she gently pulled the door shut behind her.

Leaning forward she reached across to the cold metal rail running down the wall to the bottom step and as quiet as a mouse she ventured down the wooden steps one by one, listening intently for any sounds of movement or any sign of vermin scurrying across the concrete floor.

Half way down she decided to call out and warn him of her coming;
'Hellooo', she called out gaily, but her voice sounded hollow within the silent void, 'Hello, Alf are you down here?'

As she reached the bottom of the wooden steps she stood on the cold stone cellar floor and the icy dampness of the tranquil air around her began to permeate her very bones.   She wished she'd remembered her cream angora cardigan now hanging discarded on the back of the red sofa upstairs. Her bohemian style dress, although exquisitely pretty with embroidered floral panels, hanging golden tassels and a full silk-edged skirt, was made of a thin cheesecloth material entirely unsuitable for the temperature down here and although snug and warm upstairs in the flat she was now starting to shiver quite dramatically.

She observed several tools scattered haphazardly on the floor and there was a packet of rat poison evidently being used within the trap abutting the wall but there was no sign of Alf. She cleared her throat and tentatively called his name once more.   'Alf, where are you?'   The sound of her voice reverberated against the walls.   Where was he?   Her heart began to beat faster. She wondered about the tunnel again, a little frightened remembering the vivid dream she'd had about the cellar and yet her curiosity once again overcame her fear as she moved towards the far corner. The light became dim and she saw once more the rounded edges of the bricks changing shape to form a dark recess behind them.   As before she felt herself being drawn towards it and again she called out to Alf, her voice echoing into the blackness.

Jean and Susan were busy rolling out the pastry dough on either side of the large kitchen table. They used bone handled, round ended knives to spread the softened lard evenly across the flat floury surface of the dough after which they folded it into three overlapping sections ready to roll out again. They repeated this process several times to achieve the layers of flaky pastry required for the pies.

Susan sighed, 'Oh, Jean, you probably think I'm being a bit daft but I am worried about the strange goings on in this place just recently.'

Jean stopped rolling and looked up, 'What do you mean by strange?' she looked up expectantly.

'Well, you know what I mean, these weird ghost sightings, that bizarre Cavalier fellow, and the so called 'monk' that Marian saw the other day?'

Jean laughed quietly to herself more than a little amused at Susan's obvious distress,

'Oh come on, Susan, you're letting your imagination run away with you. Marian was half joking about it and anyway she said it was dark at the time and she couldn't be sure of what she'd seen. It was probably a customer wearing a cloak or just Alf loitering in the shadows near the cellar like he often does.

Susan found herself joining in with Jean's unmistakable laughter and felt an increasing level of relief wash over her. Now that she had spoken her fears out loud she realised how silly they sounded.

'I suppose you're right', she sighed once more but smiling happily this time as she retrieved the fluted pastry cutter and got back to work. Both women continued busily rolling and cutting, rolling and cutting, on an on, making hundreds of circles, smaller ones for lids and larger ones for the base, which they then laid carefully into the dozens of greased bun tins, filling them from the enormous jar of mincemeat standing on the table. The Roberts transistor radio filled the room with music and they both hummed along to the tune 'Love me do' by the Beatles as it soothed away any tension, imagined or real.

A little later on when all the pies were in the oven cooking and Jean had gone to check on the children upstairs, Susan glanced out through the kitchen window into the garden.

Was it a trick of the light or did she see something moving in the shadows as dusk was falling, a dark figure standing by the tree. She held her breath. It was him, the same man seen by Ronnie, with the strange hat? She closed her eyes briefly opening them again as she looked out once more to the exact same place and saw nothing, only the branches swaying in the breeze; there was no one there. She needed a drink she thought. It was hot in the kitchen – she must be hallucinating!

Fiona lay still for a while. She knew she was not in her own bed, the one she was lying on now was extremely hard and uncomfortable, and the coarse mattress gave off a heady whiff of stale straw. She slowly opened her eyes and looked around the small cell-like room. It was sparsely furnished with whitewashed stone walls which were completely bare except for one large crucifix hanging high on the wall at the foot of the bed. As she studied her unfamiliar surroundings in confusion she became aware of two male voices speaking in disquieting tones on the other side of the large wooden door and she recognised Alf as one but the other voice was of a very strange dialect, possibly French, she could not discern, but she sat up shivering slightly and wrapping her arms around her knees she waited quietly, certain that all would become clear.

However, when Alf entered the room and closed the door behind him Fiona was astonished to see that he was dressed in a monk's habit. As she stared at him, looking him up and down in amazement, he also studied her in angry silence and she decided she did not like the enraged look he was giving her. She heard him exhale and curse under his breath as he slowly walked towards her.   She instinctively backed away from him but he grabbed her shoulders.

'Why did you follow me, you stupid girl, you have no idea what you have done.' He spoke in measured tones and his anger was visibly held in check.

'What are you talking about?' she queried as her heart thumped loudly in her chest. She began to feel a little nauseous and her mouth felt dry.

'Can I have a drink please?' she implored pulling free of his arms, 'I'm not feeling too great at the moment.'

Alf sighed heavily as he released her and walked over to the jug of water sitting on a small wooden table in the corner of the room.   He quickly poured her a drink and returned handing her the heavy clay-like beaker which she drank from thirstily:

Once her thirst had been sated, she looked up at him expectantly. He drew in a long breath and spoke quickly in an agitated manner.

'You followed me into the tunnel didn't you?' he said accusingly, 'I can't believe it happened like that. For years I've been trying to get through. I've tried and tried and somehow this time it was different, something changed, and for the first time it was clear. The tunnel was clear! Do you hear me? Do you know what I'm saying?'

'No!' she pleaded, 'I don't understand what you are saying. I don't know what you are talking about?' she said as she cowered away from him, trying to make sense of his outburst.

'You, you came through the tunnel with me yesterday, granted unknowingly, but you came through it nevertheless. You must have followed me down there not long after I had entered it....... I told you to stay away Fiona, I warned you. Why did you interfere?'

She frowned, looking down into the bottom of the beaker he'd given her, studying its roughened clay interior, as though she might find an answer there, to understand what he was saying to her, and then she looked up into his chiselled features, mesmerised by the icy shards within his penetrating blue eyes

'I don't remember what happened. I'm sorry if I did something wrong. I remember being in the cellar and calling out to you but I don't recall anything after that apart from waking up in this bed, here with you?'

He breathed in sharply and tried once more to take hold of the situation and to his own rising panic.

'Listen to me will you girl and I will tell you about the tunnel. The tunnel is treacherous. It was built many years ago by the Benedictine monks, and it travels from the cellar at The Pilgrims Rest right underneath Holywell Hill continuing under the shops on the other side of the street and eventually coming up under the Infirmary at the Abbey. For many years I have been trying to journey back through the tunnel but there has always been a problem. I managed to get so far but then something stopped me, a wall or barrier of some kind seemed to appear in front of me, preventing me going any further and try as I might I could not get past it. I always had to turn around and go back. But this time..... I can't believe you chose this time to come looking for me in the cellar. As soon as I realised you had followed me I returned and attempted to take you back but the tunnel began to close behind us, almost pushing us forwards in the only direction we could take, onwards and upwards. Please believe me when I tell you I could not take you back even if I had wanted to. I had no choice but to bring you here with me.'

Fiona tried to think rationally. Was he mad? Was he drunk? He was not making any sense. Somehow though Fiona did not feel he was a danger to her. He was angry and frustrated but his watery blue eyes were wide with remorse and she was not afraid of him.

'Alf, look, I'm sorry but I really don't understand what you are saying, why can't we go back, why can't we just walk across the road. If we are indeed at the Abbey, now, as you say, they will not want us here. Let's go back now. I don't feel well and I think I need to get some sleep. After the traumatic event at the lake today I think I may be having some kind of delayed shock.'

Alf looked at her pityingly for a moment and then he drew in a long breath.

'I will show you why that is not possible Fiona. Here, get these clothes on, I'm afraid they were all I could find at short notice. We will both be in serious trouble if they find you here.'

He handed her some faded black and white robes. As she unfolded them she realised with trepidation what he had given her as he quickly explained;

'A novice nun's habit will not cause any suspicion among the order. Now get dressed quickly and I will return with some food…… please do not leave this room,' he added sharply, before closing the door behind him and leaving her alone once more.

Fiona sat quietly for some time in the cold barren room. The bed was hard and comfortless and there appeared to be no heating of any kind. She quickly stood and pulled the white dress over her head pushing her arms into the long flowing sleeves letting the gown fall to the floor covering her magenta boots. She wrapped the black cloak around her shoulders, using the clasp at the front to hold it in place, and she immediately felt warmer. The white head-dress and veil fitted neatly around her head, as she carefully tucked and tamed her wild hair into the skull cap to hide it from view.   Lastly, secreted inside the pile of clothing, a rosary of wooden beads and metal links were lifted carefully over her head, a large wooden cross at its base to complete the look. She felt a little ridiculous but decided she would humour him for a while and so she sat quietly in contemplation patiently waiting for his return.

As she sat on the bed trying to gather her thoughts and martial them into some kind of order the silence was gently broken by the sound of distant and beautiful singing, like a heavenly choir, ethereal, so delicate and refined, unlike anything she had ever heard before. It moved her to such a degree that, try as she might, she could not swallow back the lump which had formed in her throat. As she touched her face she could feel the dampness of silent tears beginning to fall. With increasing unease, she quickly wiped them away, trying to get a grip.

'It will all become clear' she thought, scolding herself for becoming so emotional.

In a short while, although it had felt like an eternity to Fiona, Alf returned with some bread and wine which he placed on the wooden table.   Fiona decided that she would have preferred more water but ate and drank the wine gratefully, thinking it might help her to relax a bit. She did not realise how hungry she had been and straight away she started to feel better and her head began to clear.

She looked up to thank him and saw the concern in his eyes as she caught him examining her anxiously.

'Don't worry Alf, I'm fine now' she smiled tentatively.

'Come', whispered Alf, holding out his hand and raising her up from the bed, 'walk behind me and do not speak, just look down at the ground and never raise your eyes for a moment until I say. And I will show you something you will never believe.'

Fiona followed Alf dutifully with her head bowed low, keeping her eyes to the ground as Alf had instructed her. She was aware of her surroundings and the soft echo of their footsteps as they proceeded along a stone corridor within the Abbey. Alf stopped suddenly and spoke quietly to a man wearing a hooded cloak who stepped aside and 'allowed' them to leave the corridor through a side exit and out into what appeared to be a large courtyard.

Fiona's senses were immediately assaulted with a pungent acrid smell of urine and filth. The courtyard was bustling with people standing in groups and the area was crowded with what looked like market stalls containing wares and produce for sale.   Animals were everywhere; cows, sheep, pigs, chickens, horse drawn carts, and in one corner of the yard, she almost gasped in horror at the sight, there were rats, possibly twenty or thirty of them crawling in a scurrying group over discarded sacks of oats and wheat which had been strewn on the ground!!

Forcing herself to remain silent she followed Alf as he made his way across the courtyard. She kept her head bowed low as Alf had told her and when they reached the other side of the yard she caught sight of something she recognised, it was the well-known cedar tree outside the south transept looming up ahead of her. She thought it looked different somehow, smaller, yes, a lot smaller? But as they continued walking she looked up past the tree and along Sumpter Yard towards Holywell Hill and only then did she realise that everything in front of her had changed.

In confusion, she walked closely behind Alf and as they neared the main road she saw there were no cars, buses or traffic of any kind but only people, walking, talking, carrying their food purchases and wares in large baskets and all dressed in medieval clothing. It was like some kind of re-enactment weekend. As she looked up at the houses and buildings along either side of Holywell Hill, she stared, open mouthed at the sight of the wooden structures so different and strange looking! She gasped, unable to breathe, and Alf understanding her distress reached behind to grab her hand as the realisation dawned.

This was no re-enactment!

Alf drew her hurriedly into the small patio garden, just behind the flint wall and away from prying eyes, as he held her to him. She clung to him for comfort as the colour drained from her face. She felt faint. This couldn't be true. There must be some kind of explanation. Had she really travelled back in time with Alf, through the tunnel?

'There must be a way back' she sobbed. 'You travelled through the tunnel before didn't you?' She looked up into those clear blue eyes beseechingly. 'Please', she begged 'you must take me back.'

Alf looked at her pityingly. 'I don't know', he whispered, 'I'm not sure if it is possible again.'

'Where is the restaurant? Is it still there?' she implored and suddenly she made a desperate lunge for the street rushing on blindly as tears streamed down her face. Alf followed her as speedily as he could without drawing too much attention. Luckily her nun's habit covered her face enough that people were not aware of her anguish. She turned the corner and stumbled her way through the strange and colourless crowd of people, gradually working her way up the hill towards the restaurant. As she moved onwards and upwards she was aware that nothing was the same. The ground she walked on was no more than hardened mud, with no tarmac or paving stones of any kind to be seen. The stench was overpowering and she covered her face with her hand to quell the fumes.

The restaurant had gone or rather the place she knew had gone. Instead she saw a wooden medieval style structure with a sign swinging outside saying 'The Angel Inn.' There were no plates of scrumptious scones or fresh crusty rock cakes sitting on the shelf, hand made by Jean and Susan, just stark wooden tables and chairs sat on by strange folk in peculiar clothing breaking bread with their dirty hands and drinking ale out of pewter mugs and tankards. She sank down in despair at her plight. She had lost everything!

Alf walked up to her, aware that many people were now watching them in puzzlement, and taking her arms gently he slowly pulled her to her feet carefully manoeuvring her out of sight and into the archway.

'We need to find somewhere to stay for a while,' he decided, thoughtfully. 'Fiona, will you just listen to me for a moment' he spoke in hushed tones gently trying to break through the shock and anguish she must be feeling, 'Look, we could try the tunnel again tonight,' he said, 'when the alehouse is closed and see whether we can find our way back.'

Fiona sobbed with relief as she pleaded thankfully, 'Oh Alf, could we? I really do need to go home. I can't stay here in this place, I don't belong here. I… we need to go back, back to our own time, don't we Alf? It's so frightening here, so smelly and dirty? You don't belong here either do you…. Do you Alf?' she shook him trying to rouse him from his contemplation.

She bent down again to dab at her eyes with her sleeve, her vision unclear through a veil of tumbling tears, but as she looked up she witnessed a distinct change in his countenance. She saw in his eyes a mournful faraway gaze which deepened as he continued to look down steadfastly into her own hopeful face, swimming in fathoms of two dark liquid pools, before finally replying;

'You don't understand, do you Fiona? This is where I belong.'

He ignored her look of confusion and without speaking another word he grasped her arm and led her roughly behind him through the burgeoning throng of people who were now studying them with suspicion.   As he navigated his way efficiently across the hill he moved with determination towards the Abbey, gathering speed as he went, until Fiona was almost running to keep up with him.   As they entered the cloisters she stumbled against him as he stopped abruptly. The warmth of his body gave her immense comfort as he pulled her close to him for a moment, placing his finger against his lips to silence her, before walking on stealthily through the seemingly endless corridor thankfully devoid of any other robed figures, until at last they arrived safely back inside the cloister cell they had left only an hour or so before.

Alf closed the door securely behind him and moved with reservation to the back of the room. Not a word was spoken between them and Fiona sat for a while on the hard bed swinging her legs back and forth staring at Alf whilst he positioned himself quietly opposite her on the small wooden stool. He sat for a while clenching and unclenching his jaw in his agitation and she watched as he rubbed his fingertips in a circular motion against both temples.   She waited patiently hoping he was going to enlighten her on the words he had just spoken only a few moments before.

Finally he took a long breath and began to tell her the story he had kept hidden in his heart for almost 18 years.

Chapter Twenty One:

Reverend Jeffery sat in his office for quite a while mulling over his last conversation with Alf. He had phoned David Saunders, the Chairman of the Parochial Church Council, to discuss the problem with him and whether this matter could be added to the Agenda at the next PCC Meeting.   The Chairman had listened to the story and in no uncertain terms had quickly proceeded to tell Reverend Jeffery that this was definitely not a matter for the Council.

'My dear Jeffery, he has come to you for help. He is one of your parishioners.   If this man is mentally deranged, you should have contacted the local authorities a long time ago. He may be a danger to himself or others. I am afraid this is your responsibility and something you need to deal with.'

Jeffery had received many visits from Alf over the years. He'd indulged and patronised him, listening to his stories with only half an ear, believing him to be a little simple minded. As to whether there was any truth in Alf's assertions? He didn't think so. He had dismissed the stories all these years as the ramblings of a local loony, judging Alf to be on a par with the lost souls he visited once a fortnight at Hill End Hospital. He always demonstrated sympathy and pity for their plight but inwardly he despised them for their futility. This time though, he felt uneasy. There was something different about Alf. On previous occasions he had always shuffled into the room, his head bowed with the odd furtive sideways glance as he mumbled and stumbled over his crazy stories, but today he had a determination in his gaze and there was an urgency and desperation in his voice which Jeffery had not heard before.

Jeffery recalled Alf mentioning something of great value to be found within the tunnel and he found this a very interesting prospect. On reflection perhaps he should make some effort to appease the man, if only to relieve himself of any guilt. Chairman Saunders obviously expected him to take some action. He did not consider Alf to be dangerous but there was nothing to stop him investigating Alf's story of the tunnel? That couldn't do any harm could it? Yes, his mind was made up. He would visit the Abbey Muniment Room in the morning and have a good look through the archives, just to see if there was any mention of a tunnel in the Abbey's history.

As he sat quietly in his chair, sipping his expensive brandy and pondering his decision, he suddenly chuckled to himself laughing inwardly at his foolishness.

The next morning the Abbey seemed fairly quiet apart from a small morning service being held in the chantry and so Reverend Jeffery headed for the Archives.

He descended the stone steps and entered the dark crypt like room. A large rectangular wooden table and several chairs had been made available for anyone perusing the historical documents, all carefully preserved in glass cabinets around the perimeter of the room. The cold temperature visibly took his breath away and he quickly donned the essential white cotton gloves acknowledging the fact that light pollution, humidity and heat all contribute to the immediate disintegration of ancient documents.

He took the first large heavy file and sat for a while pouring over old maps and sketches. He knew about the dry parched marks on the surface of the abbey grounds where the old monastery had stood hundreds of years before but what lay underneath he could not begin to fathom. His footsteps echoed on the cold stone floor as he moved backwards and forwards discarding files and reaching for more. The next one he pondered over was called 'The *Martyrdoms of Alban and Amphibalus' by William the monk*. He knew the story well;

Following the death and martyrdom of Albanus, who was a roman citizen during the 2nd century AD, many Christians came to visit Verulamium on a pilgrimage to worship at the shrine of Saint Alban and the old monastery had been built around that time. However the earliest manuscripts he could find in the archives were dated much later than that, mostly around the 11th century AD. He sat for more than two hours trawling through the archives, finding nothing of note. Just as he was about to give up, he saw something. Within the writings of Matthew Paris, a Benedictine monk who scribed at the time of the English Civil War when Jesuit priests and royalists alike may well have required the use of an escape tunnel, he saw some wording in an old transcript which jolted him upright. It described; *'a long vaulted passage some five feet high and running a long way under the grounds.'*

Jeffery scanned the page in puzzlement and then read the words again to be sure;
'Well I never,' he muttered, 'maybe, just maybe there might be some truth in Alf's story after all?'

Jeffery left the archives taking a photo stat of the document he'd discovered to Peter King, the churchwarden. Peter was a round jolly man with a shock of white hair who'd lived in St Albans all his life but who'd only recently been persuaded to take over responsibility for the Muniment room. Seated at his desk, his head bent low over the document and his spectacles so far forward they were almost falling from the tip of his nose he nodded with interest at the relevant passage teasingly hinting about a possible underground tunnel. After he'd paused and pondered for a good few minutes he finally looked up and revealed to Reverend Jeffery that as far as he knew there was no such tunnel in existence today.

Jeffery found himself to be rather disappointed at this apparent dead end to the theory of the tunnel and he smiled rather ironically at the thought.

Peter sat and scratched his head with a ruler, whilst continuing to ponder over the possibility of a tunnel. Jeffery watched, with amusement, as his shockingly white hair almost stood to attention as he did so.

'You could try Archdeacon Paul!' Peter suggested nonchalantly, but then more animated, 'why yes, yes, of course, I should have thought of it before. Mind you he must be well into his eighties now if not older and retired from the clergy of course, but he lives in one of the retreat dwellings, a bit like an almshouse, given to retired clergy, it's a small private apartment at the back of the North Transept. I remember he always took a great deal of interest in the history of the Abbey and indeed the old monastery before it was destroyed. It's worth a try anyway. You'll probably find him at home now, in front of the fire, if you have time to pay him a visit.'

Reverend Jeffery stood up and smiled his gratitude shaking the churchwarden by the hand for all his help. Yes, he agreed there was no time like the present. He would go in search of him now and so taking his leave he headed off straight away to find the old retired Archdeacon. As he walked past the Dean's office and through the main gate he took a moment to look up at the awe inspiring Rose Window and enjoyed the play of the bright sunlight shining through it reflecting a multicoloured patchwork in his path. As he walked towards the North Transept he realised there was within him a small kernel of excitement and he hoped and prayed he would not be disappointed again as he knocked on the small arched door belonging to Archdeacon Paul.

An elderly manservant answered promptly and welcomed Reverend Jeffery into the warm, cosy sitting room where an ancient-looking Archdeacon Paul lounged comfortably in front of a fierce, crackling fire.   Once the initial pleasantries had been made the manservant fussed around them enthusiastically as he offered freshly brewed tea and his own home-made oatmeal cookies.

Finally he left them to their own devices and after a brief discussion on the weather and the falling numbers generally, a comfortable silence settled between them with only the sound of the odd chink and scraping of the cup against saucer.   They were seated opposite one another, on worn, weathered but extremely comfortable Marmont leather cigar chairs and after they'd finished their tea both continued to quietly study the glowing embers of the fire.

After several minutes Archdeacon Paul gripped the arms of his chair and with his gnarled hands he slowly pulled himself forwards leaning in towards his companion.   Visitors to his apartment were few and far between and he recognised in this particular visitor's demeanour a strange sense of anticipation.

'Well now, Reverend, what do you have on your mind?   Is there something I can help you with?' His peppered black and white eyebrows hung heavily over his spindly spectacles to such a degree that Jeffery could hardly see his eyes at all.

'I confess I have a strange story to tell you Archdeacon and I hardly know why I am here and taking up your time but I am investigating something for a parishioner of mine, named Alfred, or Alf as he calls himself.   He first came to see me many years ago.'

Reverend Jeffery proceeded to describe his predicament to Archdeacon Paul explaining the long history of Alf and his strange visits over the years.   He confessed to Paul that he had always thought Alf to be a little eccentric and that he had never believed any of his stories.   He then showed Paul a copy of the document which he had found in the archives and which he thought might prove that there had once been a tunnel under Holywell Hill all those years before. The more he talked, the more embarrassed he became, until he started to falter, finally stopping his meanderings as he glanced up at the Archdeacon who appeared to be listening intently.

'I am so sorry for wasting your time Archdeacon. I think I'm beginning to feel almost as mad as Alf but please could you put me out of my misery, do you know if there is any truth in this document at all or shall I just send Alf away again? I really do want to help him get a grip on reality.'

The Archdeacon took off his wiry spectacles which he rubbed gently with a custard coloured cloth.   Following a few moments of deliberation he looked up intently to fully focus on Reverend Jeffery's expression. The old man's eyes contained at their centre small black beads circumscribed with a thin circle of light amber, the whites of his eyes were now a yellowy-grey colour indicating his great age, but at that moment a youthful twinkle of excitement was evident.

'There is a tunnel' he announced without preamble, enjoying immensely the look of shock and surprise which was clear on Reverend Jeffery's face at the news and which he'd entirely anticipated;

'Oh, yes, yes, well I must admit I am amazed you've never heard of it?' he continued smugly, replacing his spectacles and relishing Jeffery's bewildered countenance with delight.

Jeffery sat for a moment or two in stunned silence and then the questions came stumbling and tumbling out of his mouth, one after another;

'Well I never, I feel such a fool! Where is it, how long has it been there, how could I not have known?'

'Well, well, well' the Archdeacon chuckled, 'I suppose it is possible that over the years it has been forgotten particularly if it's not been talked about. It was never open to visitors as it was considered too dangerous and so I suppose in a way there would be no reason for anyone to know about it. Come to think of it I myself haven't spoken about it for quite a number of years until today.'

He paused for a moment watching Jeffery relax back into the leather chair as he pondered the news, and then he had an idea;

'Well, Reverend, as you've come all this way I expect you would like to see it then, would you?' he added eagerly.

'Yes, yes please, I would, very much indeed' Jeffery replied with great excitement and interest sitting bolt upright in his chair again.

The Archdeacon rose slowly and painfully as he pushed himself up awkwardly out of his chair. He finally stood in a hunched position swaying slightly; his ability to stand up straight had disappeared long ago.

'Very well then', he said, without preamble, 'I will show you.'

He bent forwards, holding on to the mantelpiece, and pulled out his favourite bone-handled walking stick from the stick bin. Leaning on it stiffly he hobbled towards a small corner cupboard in the adjacent study.   Jeffery watched as he opened the cupboard door to display two rows of various sets of keys dangling from hooks. He lifted off a huge circular key ring which was about four inches in diameter and which appeared to Jeffery to be quite heavy and swinging from it was one large rusty looking key.

Jeffery stood up obediently as the old man beckoned him to follow and they left the apartment, heading north towards the

Lady Chapel. Although ninety-two and quite hunched over, once Paul started moving his old bones warmed up and he was able to walk quite swiftly with his trusty stick and Reverend Jeffery found it surprisingly difficult to keep up. A few yards further on Paul stopped, and again beckoned to Jeffery to come.

He pointed to a side entrance door which led them into a long narrow passageway adjacent to the cloisters. As they walked along it Jeffery realised that they appeared to go downwards for quite some distance. Finally at the far end of the corridor, the Archdeacon turned into a small panelled room. Jeffery entered the room in puzzlement. He felt that he had been here before and vaguely remembered using it one time for a prayer meeting when he had first arrived at the Abbey over 20 years before, the reason given to him at the time was because it was a 'quiet room' away from the noise of the visitors. He couldn't recall why he had never used it again but he hazily remembered being told that it was out of use and so he had never gone back there again. He frowned in confusion as he looked around the room while Archdeacon Paul stood quietly waiting in the corner. He had a superior smile on his face and his beady eyes studied Reverend Jeffery's expression of anticipation and puzzlement.

Finally, Paul could contain himself no longer and carefully with the side of his hand he stroked a small hidden wheel at the top of one of the panels until they both heard a distinct click. The panel swung outwards silently to reveal an ancient wooden door which appeared to be fastened shut with an elaborate black iron lock. The Archdeacon took the key from the large brass key ring he'd brought with him and placed it within the lock. As he turned it slowly a whirring sound could be heard within the strange antiquated mechanism as bolts were released one by one until eventually the door slid open. Reverend Jeffrey moved slowly forwards and peered into the darkness.   As his eyes grew accustomed to the gloomy interior he saw a shape forming behind the door. It was a circular entrance to a long dark tunnel.

He peered into the dimness, holding his breath in amazement before asking 'Where does it go?'

'Nowhere' answered the Archdeacon flatly. 'It was blocked up a few yards along many years ago but there are many stories surrounding its use. It could have been used in the Elizabethan era as a possible escape route. At that time many of the seminary priests and recusants were persecuted for their Romanist beliefs. During the Protestant reign anyone who would not take the Oath of Supremacy was likely to be imprisoned or worse. It was also thought that during the Powder Conspiracy some of the Catholics involved fled to St Albans and used the tunnel to hide and get away.'

'What are you saying?' spluttered Reverend Jeffery in disbelief 'you don't mean Guy Fawkes do you?'

Paul smirked, 'Hmm well may be not Guy Fawkes himself, but possibly members of his gang...... well, so the story goes anyway.'

'Well I never, this is astonishing,' remarked Reverend Jeffery in complete bewilderment. I really can't thank you enough Archdeacon. This has been truly enlightening! I am so glad I came to see you. I just wish I had known about this all those years ago. I am not sure whether any of this information will really help Alf but at least I can go back to him now and let him know that the tunnel he has been telling me about really does exist and it may well have been here for many centuries. As to his claim that he came through it all those years ago well that may be a bit harder to swallow.'

Chapter Twenty Two:

'I remember running into the tunnel during the siege of the Abbey' recounted Alf, turning away from Fiona's searching eyes and confused look, his pain palpable to her as his story began to unfold. 'The King's soldiers were herding people together into groups using their horses as battering rams, "If you love your King, then show him your love" the soldiers demanded, "hand over your gold and your treasure." People were screaming and running in all directions, not sure which way to run for safety.'

Alf paused and sat down on the stool in the corner of the room.

He looked down at his worn and leathered hands, interlocking his fingers as he recalled the youthful hands of the young boy who'd run into the tunnel that fateful day, that momentous day when for the second time in his short life his whole world had been turned upside down. He wiped the corner of his wet eyes with the top of his sleeve at the memory of it, and the injustice. What had he done to deserve such misery? His memories of that frightful experience started to become more vivid and his eyes were widened with renewed dread.

'Tell me', Fiona prompted him gently. 'Tell me what happened to you Alf' she encouraged as she watched and waited for him to continue.

Alf breathed in deeply and spoke solemnly once more.

'The tunnel was well known to me for I had used it many times when fetching wine from the cellar located at the end of the tunnel. It was stored in the cool darkness where it matured over many years, some bottled from grapes grown in the vineyards around the monastery and the rest imported from France and Germany such as Claret, Madeira, Sherry, and Hock. There were hundreds of bottles stored down there, some of it was used for the liturgy but much of it was served as part of the everyday meals provided to the monastic community.

On this occasion I was frantically trying to hide from the King's men. They wouldn't find me down there, I thought, I would be completely safe. I could hide secretly behind the rows of bottles, there was plenty of food and drink available to me; bread, cheese and wine, I could last for a few days if I had to. I had intended to come back of course, once everything had quietened down. I remember jogging through the tunnel as I had many times before but I sensed something was different and half way through it I stood for a while in the shadows feeling a little lost and disorientated. And then, as I continued moving slowly forwards through the unfamiliar passageway my senses began reeling with a strange pungent smell which almost overpowered me but finally I found myself in an area I recognised which was right outside the cellar.

I waited for a while listening to see if anyone had followed me but I could hear nothing. In the stillness I reached for the latch to the cellar door but it just wasn't there, I searched and searched, groping for it in the darkness but couldn't find it and instead my hand felt the smooth damp surface of the cellar wall. As I entered the cellar I knew something was not right, the room was completely different, it was changed in every way imaginable. The wooden racks containing rows and rows of bottles which usually lined the walls were now gone, seemingly vanished into thin air? Instead the cellar was cluttered with piles of unfamiliar cardboard boxes which I then clambered over to make my way out of the cellar and on up the wooden steps to the door at the top, all the while assuming I would re-emerge out of the cellar door and into the ale house. Of course when I arrived at the top it wasn't the ale house at all, it was.........., well, you know the rest!   At the time I thought I must be dreaming or I'd hit my head on something in the tunnel. I was sure that everything would soon become clear? I made my way furtively through the side corridor and into the garden and then I walked out through the gate ending up under the archway where my world collapsed around me.

Once I realised my dilemma I sat down and curled myself into a tight ball hoping the nightmare would go away. I remember sobbing and banging my head repeatedly against the damp wall beneath the archway where I stayed for a long time with my eyes tight shut until your Nana Win found me, a snivelling wreck.'

Fiona stared at his bowed head trying to take in all that he had told her. Her mind rejected the implausibility of it and yet it was all too real. It must be true. Her heart went out to him as she tried to imagine what it must have been like to live for all those years in such isolation and despair.

'My God, Alf, how dreadful! What an incredible story and who would ever believe it? No one in their right mind, and yet here I am now, and so I must believe it but I'm fighting against it with all my reasoning and rationality. If I hadn't seen it with my own eyes I would definitely think you a madman. I also recognise that strange smell you are talking about, I can't quite describe it, it's alien, unfamiliar and pungent, but definitely overpowering and disturbing!'

She stood and paced backwards and forwards in the small space available.

Her distress was palpable and Alf watched as she pulled back her headdress and removed her skull cap, rubbing at her temples to soothe away her unease. She pulled out the comb which held her soft brown hair aloft and let it tumble down around her shoulders. She ruffled and massaged her mane, pulling forward long strands which she twisted around her fingers, leaving the rest to swing loose at the back, long and heavy. It swayed in rippling waves as she continued to walk to and fro, and all the while Alf couldn't take his eyes off her, dumbstruck, in awe, unable to put into words the emotion he was feeling at that moment, knowing that he yearned with all his heart to reach out and touch her, to pull her down into his arms and physically comfort her.

Fiona stopped pacing and secured her hair once more; winding it around and on top of her head all the while trying to make sense of their predicament.

Sighing deeply she turned to face Alf, speaking her thoughts out loud. 'I am so sad for you Alf, when I think back over the years, I always knew there was some sort of mystery surrounding you, the way you kept yourself to yourself, never mixing with anyone and all the time I just thought you were a loner, and I hate to admit it, a loser, but who could ever have guessed you were harbouring a secret like this! Everything makes sense now. I am so sorry.'

She crouched down on her knees in front of him. Finding his hands she held them in her own.

'And no one knew your secret? Oh how I wish I had made more of an effort to talk to you through all of those friendless years. I despise myself for that.'

Alf felt the warmth of her hands and as he looked into her soft, compassionate eyes he suddenly realised a great feeling of relief. She believed him utterly and without doubt. He now knew he was not alone in his nightmare, someone else knew and understood.

'There is just one other person I have told' he admitted. 'After a few months of my arriving at The Pilgrims Rest - a rather appropriate sanctuary for my situation, don't you think?' he said smiling sadly, the irony not lost on either of them. 'I contemplated that perhaps some godly intervention had occurred and brought me here to this place of refuge, it was my destiny and therefore important that I should not leave my safe haven.

I was content with that notion for a while and busied myself with errands and tasks for your Nana Win, however one day when I was sweeping the steps above the shop I overheard a table full of customers discussing their visit to the Abbey and, as I listened to their chatter, I realised that I was literally only a stone's throw away from it, and so surely, I reflected, I might be able to find some answers there.

Reverend Jeffery was only a young curate then and seemed keen to listen to me and my story. He seemed to understand my pain. He suggested that I should stay at the restaurant for the time being and said he would make some investigations about the tunnel. I don't know if he really believed my story at the time. I went back several times after that but each time he assured me there was no tunnel and he urged me to resume my life at the restaurant. I left it for a few years, trying to do as he asked but recently I went back to him again. I was concerned about you. I realised that night when I carried you back to your bed that you probably had your suspicions. I was worried something like this might happen. The Reverend reassured me yet again saying that he would investigate once more but I had the feeling he thought I was either insane or a liar. I hoped but was not convinced that he believed me.'

Fiona stood and walked back to the wooden bed and sighed heavily as she sat down.

'No Alf, I'm sorry but I don't think he did believe you. I'm afraid I heard him on the phone after you had left his office, he was talking to someone about you – I believe he thought you deluded?

Alf looked at her in astonishment, his mouth wide open, as a fish gasping for air. Then he closed his lips together tersely, and frowned.

'How do you know that? Were you there? Did you follow me to the Abbey?' he queried sharply.

She returned his gaze guiltily,

'Yes, I did Alf. I'm so sorry; I shouldn't have done it but I just wanted to know what was going on.'

He stared at her in confusion and dismay. Could he have been more careful? He'd tried to tell her to stay away but should he have made more of an effort to warn her, to be more explicit, and prevent this from happening? He studied her hangdog expression, her aura of loss and confusion, and relenting a little he decided that he could not have said anything further to her that would have kept her away, not without raising suspicion anyway. Sadly he realised it had been her youth and naivety which had led her to this place.

'Well I hate to say it' replied Alf sarcastically, 'but now you do know what's going on and just look where that has gotten you?' He groaned aloud in his anguish and disapproval, 'I tried to warn you but you just didn't listen.'

Her eyes misted again as they sat in silence for a while both trying to hold on to some sort of logic about their situation.

Suddenly Alf gasped and moved quickly towards the door.

'Fiona, listen to me will you, I want you to stay here for a short while, I need to do something of great importance and then I will return, I promise. Please just remain here in this room quietly and you should be fine, ok?'

Fiona nodded silently in sombre acquiescence.

As he closed the heavy door behind him Fiona sat down on the straw bed once more. She felt utterly spent following the roller coaster ride she'd endured during the last few hours, the extremes of emotion she'd experienced had left her drained and tearful, and she hoped Alf wouldn't be gone too long. Fear and foreboding for this alien environment was uppermost in her mind. After a few moments peaceful solitude the pounding in her chest seemed to subside a little in his absence and the silence within the cave like room enveloped her. She felt thankful in a way to have this short respite and was determined to gather her senses so that reason might prevail.

Alf moved silently along the corridor, scolding himself for his stupidity. Why he had almost forgotten the reason he was here. This was the triumphant moment he'd been waiting and longing for and now he needed to seize this opportunity to find the sword and take it back with him through the tunnel. The girl was a distraction he could well do without; she had completely taken over his thoughts!

When Alf had first arrived at the monastery all those centuries ago, a lost and lonely lad, defeated and desperate, he had pounded on the huge bronze door for what seemed like an eternity and it had been William, the Prior Monk, who had come to his aid that night. His friendly face had appeared, like a beam of light, from behind the small grated peephole, and on seeing the wretched youth he'd immediately pulled open the heavy door and welcomed him in to the monastery. He had been the gentle giant who from then on had happily taken Alf under his wing, and it was William who had first entranced him with the story of the martyrdom of St Alban.

In the year 283 AD, Albanus, a kindly townsman of adequate income, had given shelter to a priest fleeing persecution for his Christian faith. During his stay Albanus had watched the priest, whose name was Amphibalus, and so impressed was he by the faith and piety shown by Amphibalus, that he found himself emulating the priest and soon afterwards Albanus himself converted to Christianity. When Roman soldiers were sent to the house to arrest the priest for blasphemy Albanus wanted to protect Amphibalus and so he covered himself in the priest's cloak so that the soldiers would take him instead, which they did.

Albanus was sent before the judge Maximius, a Pagan who, when he realised his mistake, tried to persuade Albanus to worship the pagan god Phoebus and all would be forgiven but Albanus stood fast to his new found faith saying loudly 'I worship and adore the true and living God who created all things.'

This enraged the judge who ordered Albanus scourged thinking that a whipping would shake the constancy of his heart but Albanus bore these torments patiently and joyfully. When the judge realized that these tortures would not shake his faith, he ordered that Albanus be beheaded and so he was taken to the hill top where the beheading was to take place. It is said that Albanus felt a strong thirst come over him and miraculously a well sprung up nearby giving the martyr a drink. The executioner, on seeing this miracle, dropped to his knees and begged forgiveness from Albanus renouncing his pagan god and saying that he would worship the Christian god for ever more and that he would not behead Albanus.

But salvation for Albanus was short lived for immediately a replacement executioner was found who picked up that same sword and slayed Albanus on command. As Albanus' head was severed from his body, it bounced and rolled all the way down the hill to the bottom and where it stopped another well sprung up. At this point the executioner started wailing and after dropping the sword he covered his face with his hands, as blood started spurting through his fingers and his eyes fell from their sockets.

In the ensuing chaos Amphibalus, who had been watching the proceedings whilst hidden amongst the crowd, gathered up the sword and when he saw his saviour's body being wrapped in sack cloth he begged the crowd to release it to him. They allowed him to move forward and as he crouched over the still form he made the sign of the cross and gathering him up he carried him down the hill. A while later the head of Albanus was brought to Amphibalus by a roman soldier who swung it irreverently by the hair backwards and forwards. He called out to Amphibalus saying, 'hey you take this,' and he threw it towards the priest and where it landed a river sprung up, the River Ver, meaning 'truth' and thereafter the area was called Verulamium. When the judge heard about these miracles he was very afraid and ordered further persecutions to cease and he declared Albanus to be a saint and that all should honour him.

Alf's heart sang when he found the sword in the exact same spot where he'd buried it not long before Henry's soldiers had arrived at the monastery and he'd fled to the tunnel for safety. He calculated, looking at the state of the freshly dug earth, that the sword had only been buried a few hours before. They had literally travelled back through the tunnel and arrived within twenty four hours or so of the time he had left it. He had come back to his own time and realised he should be relieved but strangely he felt no comfort at the thought. All he could think about was Fiona and his responsibility to her. He must try his utmost to return her to her family and the only way to do that was to head back through the tunnel. He quickly retrieved the sword, smoothing over the earth, and made his way back to the room where he had left her.

As he walked past the scriptorium he looked in through the open doorway and saw the familiar bowed head of his friend and mentor, William. A feeling of anguish akin to physical pain flooded his body as he realised he couldn't go to him, to warn him, this would be impossible! He was almost twenty years older than the last time they had seen each other, how could he explain that to his old friend? He wracked his brains quickly and thankfully an idea came to him; there was indeed something he could do! He remembered the messaging system whereby townsfolk could pass messages through from the outside world and into the monastic community. He could use this system as a way to warn William of the impending raid. He quickly entered the outer parlour and scribbled a note. He then sealed it with wax and left it in the message box.

It read:

Search by soldiers imminent. Take everything and leave – A friend.

'Oh Alf, there you are, I was starting to get worried', Fiona said anxiously as Alf reappeared. 'What have you got there?'

Alf shut the door carefully behind him and quickly covered the sacred artefact beneath his robe so it was hidden from view. He was relieved that she was alright and had not been discovered.

'It is a very important Christian relic' he explained, 'it is the sacred sword used to behead the first Christian martyr, Saint Alban. I need to keep it with me and bring it back to its rightful resting place in the Abbey within the shrine of Saint Alban.'

'I don't understand, questioned Fiona, 'why can't you put it in the shrine here, now?'

'Because it is not safe here!' he replied impatiently.

'Don't you see, if I can get it back through the tunnel, back to 'The Pilgrims Rest', it will be safe for generations to come. I know that the shrine survives because I've seen it in the future, in your time, but all the other artefacts were taken and no-one knows for sure where they are now?'

'But why is it so important? After all it's just a sword, isn't it? I mean, it's not even a nice thing to have. It chopped off the head of a saint for goodness sake. Why do you want to keep it?'

Alf stood in silence for a while contemplating how much information he could or should share with her. Finally he responded briefly and in a quiet, thoughtful voice;

'May be I'll tell you one day'

Although she was intrigued and a little confused, Fiona changed the subject.

'Ok fine, but how long will it be before we can go back?' she asked anxiously.

Alf frowned, placing his free hand firmly on her shoulder as he leant in towards her. He held her gaze for several seconds before he replied seriously, 'Fiona just listen to me will you? I am so sorry to have to tell you this but to be honest with you I really don't know whether we can ever go back.'

He watched her young innocent face change from a look of feverish animation to one of fear and impending doom, and he added quickly;

'But we have to try, ok? We will wait for darkness to fall and then we will make our way to the north wall of the nave....... I think I remember now; that is where the old tunnel entrance lies.'

Chapter Twenty Three:

After Archdeacon Paul had pulled the secret door back into position, whereby it locked itself via an ingenious and impressive mechanism of cogs, wheels and shunts, Reverend Jeffery escorted Archdeacon Paul back to his chambers. Once they arrived outside his door Jeffery shook the Archdeacon's hand at length, thanking him profusely for enlightening him on the existence of the old tunnel. Paul grew weary of his attentions and thought of his comfortable leather armchair by the fire.

'Would you mind very much if I held on to the key,' Jeffery implored the Archdeacon beseechingly. 'I would dearly love to see the look on Alf's face when I show him the room and what is secreted within.'

Paul's already deeply furrowed brow creased a little more as his small beady eyes rested on Reverend Jeffery's earnest expression. His reticence was apparent as his grip tightened on the brass ring he was holding. The ancient key dangling from it had been in his keeping for more than fifty years. It had never been out of his possession.

'I promise I will return it to you by late afternoon tomorrow' reassured Reverend Jeffery.

Paul thought for a moment and then growing weary with the conversation he shrugged his narrow bony shoulders and handed it over to the younger man.

'Just until tomorrow then', the Archdeacon acquiesced obligingly.

Reverend Jeffery gleefully grasped the large heavy key ring and casually slipped it inside the secret opening of his cassock. In obvious delight he shook hands vigorously with Paul for one last time before turning to leave.

'Goodbye, and thanks again for your time and trouble' he repeated as he walked away, the sound of his voice and footsteps echoing in the now emptying church.

A few seconds later Jeffery looked back over his shoulder to give Paul a small wave but the Archdeacon had already disappeared inside his warm cosy apartment closing the door firmly behind him, and locking it to ward off any more intruders. He decided he'd had quite enough activity for one day.

Jeffery walked quickly towards the main chancel and his office. He was half way there when he slowed down and came to a halt. He stood for a moment rubbing his chin in thought as an idea took hold. He smiled secretly to himself and eventually he swivelled on his heel heading off in another direction entirely; back towards the quiet room.

There appeared to be no one about as visitors to the Abbey had mostly gone home now and so he arrived quickly at his destination. He walked over to the corner where the Archdeacon had previously stood almost gloating in his superior knowledge, and he soon found the secret wheel on top of the panelling. His heart was thumping with excitement as the old door concealing the tunnel entrance was revealed to him once more. He turned the key gingerly in the lock and peered into the darkness cursing himself for not being more organised and bringing a torch. He should probably go back and get one but his curiosity got the better of him and he clambered inside.

'I'll just go in a short way' he thought to himself as he pulled the door to behind him and moved slowly forwards on his knees.

About twenty yards in he came to a sudden stop as he realised a panel of wood appeared to have been lodged between two stone-like bricks completely blocking his way. He pressed against it with both hands trying to see if it would move at all which in fact it did.   He realised it was not cemented in but merely propped up in the grooves of the stones. He shifted the wood from side to side manipulating the edge of it until suddenly one side became free and the whole thing fell forwards with a thud echoing loudly ahead of him down the length of the tunnel.

Beyond he could see the passageway widened and the roof was a bit higher. He moved forward a little further and then managed to get up off his knees and walk along in a stooped manner. Gradually as he moved further along he found he could stand up a little straighter and walk without too much difficulty. A light seemed to be shining in the distance but he could not make out where it was coming from. As he walked along, incredulous, he sensed that perhaps he should not be there, that he was an intruder, but somehow he felt unable to turn back.

He speculated, what was it Alf had said?   That there was something of value down here. Was it a stash of money or treasure of some kind he wondered?   Unexpectedly he stumbled upon something soft. He looked down and saw what looked like a pile of old clothes. As he bent down he could just make out an old black cloak. As he lifted it up from the ground it almost disintegrated in his hands, like a dead moth, turned to powder. He searched the area for anything else of interest and found nestled in the rocks nearby a large brimmed felt like hat which looked like something out of the history books. 'Well well well', he thought, wondering how many aeons had passed since the last person had travelled along this route.

Could these remnants have been left by one of Guy Fawkes' men as he fled through the tunnel to safety? He was fascinated by the concept. Maybe the chap had hidden other items, gems perhaps, or a stash of gold coins. If so, they could be worth a fortune! He decided to explore a little further along the dark, dank passageway heading towards the light. As he moved further on through the gloom he began to inhale a strange pungent aroma which aroused in him a feeling of nausea making him close his eyes and sway against the side wall of the tunnel. His nostrils flared in discomfort as he clung on to the rough stones for support and he started to contemplate turning back. Groaning inwardly he opened his eyes in confusion as he peered straight into the mouth of a second tunnel entrance which had just opened up, almost mirage like, to the left of the original.

What should he do now, which way should he go? A rational thought also persisted, should he turn back? As he stood for a moment and recovered from his weakness the compulsion to follow the tunnel to his left became overpowering. Slowly he moved forward towards the light in the distance which seemed to beckon him onwards. As he got closer to it the strange smell returned and he could hear voices shouting in the distance.

He felt a gnawing disappointment at the realisation that he must have come across another exit and therefore had found nothing of any interest within the tunnel. Keen to breathe in some fresh air he emerged from the dark into the sudden brightness of the outside world. He stood for a moment in speechless incredulity as he looked around him.

With profound fear coursing through his veins at the sight he turned around quickly to make his escape only to watch the

remains of the tunnel entrance disappearing into the rocks
behind him.

Chapter Twenty Four:

Joe Saville, the tobacconist, picked up his old iron lamp and entered his cellar to check for rats. Alf had told him there were dozens of the blighters but he'd never seen any. He held up his lamp, slowly moving it from side to side as he tried to see into the farthest corners of the cold dark room. He began tutting and swearing under his breath as he realised the lamp was running out of oil. He sniffed at the air and breathed in a strange sweet smell which made him feel a little light headed and he wondered what it might be? It wasn't the lamp he was sure of that.

As he surveyed the cellar he could see an area in the corner where Alf had been working. Alf had obviously moved some furniture and cleared a space near the wall. As Joe moved closer he saw a makeshift trap door with a large circular iron ring at its centre which appeared to have been scored into the floor boards.   How strange, he thought to himself, sure in his own mind that he had never seen it before and he'd lived here for over thirty years!

Inquisitively he moved towards the trap door and crouching down he placed his lamp on the ground next to it. He pulled gently at the iron ring until the large square section of the floor was loosened. As he pulled it a little more it shifted and lifted up like the lid on a gift box. He carefully propped it on its side leaning it carefully against the wall and then he leant forward and peered down into the hole.

He could see a number of old stone steps worn away over time with deep indentations in the middle of each step.

'Well I never, that's crazy' he muttered to himself, 'I never knew this was here.' He scratched his head in confusion 'may be this is where the rats are?' he wondered.

With some trepidation he picked up his lamp and slowly descended the steps, still wearing his comfy mule like slippers, and he shone the lamp ahead of him into the darkness.   He could feel the dampness in the air as he carefully stepped down off the last step and looked about him. To his left and right, there was nothing but old brick walls but ahead and in front of him he could see a long dark tunnel which disappeared into the distance.

He was mystified trying to get his bearings as to where it could possibly lead when suddenly he heard faint echoes of voices and footsteps coming towards him.   Beads of sweat appeared on his forehead as he peered into the darkness. His hands grew clammy, and his mouth and tongue became dry. He tried hard to swallow but failed and became transfixed watching in the distance as two ghostly hooded figures appeared from the gloom. His heart started pounding as the apparition grew nearer and he cried out in fear as he sank down onto the damp floor and into oblivion as, shrouded in mist, the monk and the nun came into view.

'It's Mr Saville' gasped Fiona in realisation and Alf nodded knowingly.

'Yes, we'd better get him back up into the shop quickly before he comes round.

'Oh, Alf, do you realise what this means?' she cried clutching at his sleeve. 'We're back, back in our own time, Oh thank God, thank God' she sobbed falling on to Alf in gratitude.

Alf held her to him for a brief moment and then gathered her up to face him. He gave her a solemn look and shook her firmly before speaking to her sternly, 'Yes, we're back but Fiona you must listen to me, we need to keep all of this a secret ok? Please promise me, you won't say anything to anyone.'

He smoothed away her tears of joy with his cloak and hugged her to him again as she nodded her agreement.

'Ok Alf, whatever you say. I'm just so glad to be home.'

Alf bent down to check on the old man who was still slumped in a heap on the floor where he'd fallen at the entrance to the tunnel.

'He seems ok, his breathing is fine, he must have just fainted with the shock I think, come here would you and help me lift him?'

Fiona wiped her face quickly and together they managed to haul the unconscious tobacconist up the steps and back into his cellar. Alf closed the trap door and moved the heavy trunk back over it, just in time to hear Mr Saville mumbling something about ghosts in the cellar. Fiona quickly removed her robe and Alf stepped out of his cloak just as Mr Saville opened his eyes.

'W w where am I, w what happened to me? Did I have a fall?' Mr Saville rubbed the side of his face where a slight bruise was forming. 'I s saw 'em down there, g g ghosts!'

Fiona and Alf exchanged a brief transient glance then quickly smiled their reassurances to Joe confirming he'd just suffered a slight fall in the cellar with no ill effect and that imagination can sometimes play tricks on you. Joe was acquiescent and decided he quite enjoyed the fuss being made of him as they helped him into the room at the back of the shop leaving him with a cup of warm cocoa sitting in his armchair in front of the TV.

As they emerged from the newsagents shop and closed the door behind them everything was as it should be.

The noisy road was filled with cars and buses and Fiona was content to wait for the busy traffic to stop at the traffic lights. Never again would she curse the constant flow of cars as they motored up the hill. She gratefully limped across to the other side of the street with Alf following behind carrying the precious sword heavily wrapped in coarse sacking.

'How long have we been gone?' queried Fiona, 'will they have been worried about us do you think?'

'I'm not sure', it's probably not been that long, but perhaps you'd better have a story ready just in case' suggested Alf.

As they walked up the street towards the restaurant Fiona looked up and saw her mother at the shop door, turning the sign around from 'open' to 'closed.' She waved as she caught her mother's eye and Alf quickly took the opportunity to dart into the archway walking up the short slope and into the back garden as fast as he could while Fiona continued up the hill to the shop doorway where her mum was standing, waiting for her.

 'Hello mum', she gulped trying not to cry 'have you been wondering where I was?'

'Well, yes, I was starting to get a little worried,' Jean admitted as she took in her washed-out appearance. 'Where have you been? Was that Alf with you?'

'Oh, yes, I bumped into him coming up the hill' she said, lying a bit too easily as she reached out and hugged her mum to her, almost too hard, breathing in the smell of her, 'Oh mum, mum, it's so lovely to be home.'

Although Jean was a little startled and surprised at this unusual show of affection which was usually reserved for Dougie she hugged her eldest daughter to her kissing her hair;

'Well I never, I can't remember the last time you gave me a cuddle like that' she said pleasurably, 'now hurry up and get your things together, we'll be heading home soon.'

On reaching the sanctuary of his bedroom Alf closed the door behind him and leaned back against it. He closed his eyes for a few moments to embrace the familiar sensation and aura of his own private space. His breathing was heavy and his heart thumped loudly in his chest but a strong feeling of relief seemed to wash over him and he felt profoundly grateful to have returned safely to the Pilgrims Rest and back to his own room once more. He realised then, for the first time in nearly 20 years, he'd come home.

Moving deftly he sat himself down on the bed cautiously balancing the well wrapped sword gently across his lap.

Carefully and reverently he unbound the sack cloth to reveal the treasured artefact. As he held the ivory handle of the roman gladius firmly in his left hand, he proceeded to wipe away all traces of dust from the blade with his soft white handkerchief. He admired the sword's workmanship, and kissed the blade tenderly like a long lost friend. Then he stood and laid the sword softly along the length of the bed. Kneeling down he held the sword firmly as he gently twisted the wooden pommel at the top of the handle. It was stiff and grimy but as he gently pulled and manipulated it within the palm of his hand, it began to move. He twisted and tugged at the pommel, until it loosened and suddenly came away in his hand.

He smiled with satisfaction as he looked inside the hollow crevice and carefully pulled out the piece of parchment lodged within.   He whispered the words 'gratias ago tibi, domine' and thanked God that his journey had not been in vain.   With the utmost care he slowly and reverently opened out the faded vellum and scrutinised the ancient map before him.

Chapter Twenty Five:

Ronnie stomped into the kitchen with a scowl on his face. Jean was sitting having a cup of tea and looked up as she heard him enter.

'Oh my goodness Ronnie, whatever is the matter' she asked worriedly.

Ronnie drew in a deep breath and then wretchedly demanded;

'Who the devil is this Cavalier feller? Susan thinks she's seen him now! Is he a ghost or just a pest? We need to find out once and for all. I haven't managed to get a good look at him yet but he seems to like hanging around that tree in the garden; I feel as though he's watching and waiting for something, but I don't know what for?'

Ronnie shakily lit a cigarette and Jean watched him thoughtfully. There were no customers about, they'd all gone home after the lunches and all the food had been put away so she considered it was probably a good idea for him to have a smoke and perhaps it would help him to wind down.

As he sucked in long and hard he waited for the familiar lightheaded euphoria to arrive but it didn't come as his breath suddenly caught in his lungs. After emitting a horrible rasping sound, he started to cough violently and his whole body shook with the force of it. His coughing quickly changed to choking and he couldn't seem to stop long enough to draw breath.

Jean was horrified as she realised he needed help. She quickly got up from her stool and in a panic she ran to the sinks in the scullery to fetch him a glass of water. Her heart was pounding. It was so frightening to see him in that state. As Ronnie gurgled and spluttered, his face turned red and then almost purple in colour. He grabbed his hankie from his trouser pocket and quickly wiped his mouth. He looked down in dismay at the ring of putrid blood contained within it and quickly stuffed it back into his pocket, not wanting Jean to see it, and then he collapsed down on to the kitchen floor where he lay wheezing and spent as his coughing gradually subsided.

As he tried to calm himself and recover sufficiently enough to pull himself back up he was overcome by a feeling of dread. He knew that his lungs were beginning to fail him again and his time was running out. He tried to console himself.

'I've done well' he thought 'I've seen my kids grow up, I've provided for them. I've been there for them. I couldn't have asked for more. I could have died years ago, like all those other poor sods!'

He remembered the first time he'd seen the blood in his handkerchief. It had been thirty years before and he'd been 25. At the time he hoped it was going to be nothing serious but the doctor had sent him for an immediate X-ray and the result had been devastating; Tuberculosis on his right lung. In those days the treatment endured by the patient was to do absolutely nothing, to have complete bed rest and basically to behave just like a log!

And so that's what Ronnie did. He was sent away to a Sanatorium and he did just that, hardly moved at all for several months, following doctors' orders.

He was allowed to get up once a day after three months and sit in a chair. And then gradually over the following three months the signs on his door would change. Firstly he went on to 'basins' which meant he could wash himself in his own room, and then 'OTW' which meant out to wash, where he could walk to the end of the corridor and use the bathroom. Then the signs switched to '1 hour up' then '2 hours up' to '3 hours up' and so on. Things seemed to be going well until, at the end of the longest six months of his life, he haemorrhaged once more during another coughing fit and a further X-ray showed a cavity had formed in his lung. In the end there was no alternative and surgical intervention was his only option. Ronnie underwent a lobectomy and the diseased part of his lung was taken away. Even now he could remember vividly the dreadful gnawing pain in his chest following the operation. Day and night he could get no relief. It was as if an iron fist had been plunged inside his ribs tearing out his very soul leaving him miserable and empty and whatever position he sought to adopt he had found it impossible to sleep comfortably for many weeks afterwards.

The slow recuperation following his operation meant another three months' stay in hospital and then eventually he had been allowed to come home.

The specialists had done all they could. They instructed him to resume his life, wishing him well, washing their hands of him, but Ronnie knew deep inside his prognosis was not good, his life would never be the same, and he knew he had not been cured.

He married his sweetheart, Susan, who had waited for him loyally and patiently throughout his illness, and together they had three healthy children who he'd been able to watch grow and thrive. It had saddened him at times that he couldn't run or play sports with them like other fathers, or be able to throw them up in the air and catch them when they were small, or play football with his boys as they got older, but his consolation was that he could provide for them. Every day he worked in the kitchen and helped to run the family business. He was aware that his brother Dougie probably did more than his fair share of the heavy chores but there was a silent agreement that Ronnie could go upstairs to rest if he needed to and the fear of his symptoms returning was his constant companion.

Jean arrived back with the water and held the glass to his lips as he drank gratefully. She found herself unable to speak whilst he continued to take small sips from the glass. As she cradled his head she found herself concentrating on the rise and fall of his chest. She listened to the gurgling sounds gradually subside as his breathing slowed a little. After a while she helped him up to his feet and manoeuvred his weight on to the chair next to the table.

'I'll go and get help' she said, as she made him comfortable putting her cardigan around his shoulders. He sat very still and said nothing.

'I'll find Susan' she said to him. 'You take it easy and sit here for a while.' Ronnie nodded, not wanting to speak again in case he started coughing once more. He sat quietly on the high wooden chair at the kitchen table. The pain in his chest started to ease and he began to feel a little better.

As he looked out into the garden his eyes misted and he blinked and rubbed them in alarm. Once again the cloaked figure was standing there leaning against the lilac tree. As George watched him the cavalier slowly raised his gloved hand to his mouth and removed the lit cheroot he had been smoking. He threw it down under his boot and ground it out decisively. After a few seconds he turned and raising his hand to the brim of his hat he gave Ronnie a brief nod.

Archdeacon Paul waited for Reverend Jeffery to return the key the following afternoon. He started to become a little anxious by about 6 pm when he had not arrived and with immense irritation at being 'put out' he found his walking stick and decided to go and collect it himself. He asked Peter the curate for the whereabouts of Reverend Jeffery's office and eventually after being shown the way he stood in front of the heavy oak door marked 'Private' and knocked on it with his stick. He listened for a moment but on hearing no reply he tried the handle carefully and finding it to be unlocked he entered the surprisingly lavish room. There was no sign of Reverend Jeffery only an old unwashed coffee cup sitting on his desk.

'Hmm' muttered Paul to himself, becoming concerned.

'Where the devil has he got to? I think I might check out the tunnel and make sure there is nothing amiss here?'

Peter, the curate who had been hovering in the corridor, requested permission to accompany Paul to the quiet room as he was extremely curious about the so-called secret tunnel. Paul had no objection and they both walked together amiably along the narrow passageway adjacent to the cloisters. On entering the small room at the end they both immediately saw that the door to the tunnel was slightly ajar.

Peter chuckled loudly in surprise at the sight of it and scratched his head in disbelief.

'Well, well, and there I was telling Reverend Jeffery there was no tunnel. I was so sure of it and yet here it is for all to see!'

'Yes, well that's all very well and good' Paul explained in annoyance, 'but look at this carelessness, the man has left it unattended and I specifically asked him to return the key to me today.'

He walked across the room to the opening and peered inside. After a moment he turned round to Peter with concern on his face.

'You don't suppose he went in there do you?

Peter smirked and then proceeded to shake his head and tut, 'Well let's face it; he wouldn't have got very far along would he? It was only a few minutes ago that you'd just finished telling me how it's all been boarded up in there for years for safety reasons, weren't you?'

'Yes, yes, of course it is, silly me. He must have just left it open. I'll shut it up now and return the key to its proper place. If he wants to have another look he'll have to come and get the key from me again. Thank you for all your help Peter, I think I'd better return to my quarters now, I need a rest after all this rushing about!' he groaned and rubbed his aching back as he hobbled across the floor once more and out of the room.

Before leaving, Peter looked around the room once again. With the door shut and the panelling back in place there was no sign of a tunnel existing in this room at all. No wonder he hadn't known about it, he thought, chuckling to himself once more before he turned off the lights and shut the door firmly behind him. He walked jauntily down the corridor whistling the tune from his favourite hymn;

'He who would valiant be 'gainst all disaster, let him in constancy, follow the Master.
There's no discouragement shall make him once relent his first avowed intent...... to be a pilgrim.'

****

Once they arrived home, Ronnie recounted his ordeal to Susan. He sat in his comfy red velveteen armchair which overlooked his beloved garden, a calming cup of tea in his hands, and all seemed normal again.

'I was so frightened Susan, my love, I couldn't breathe! It's my lungs; they're giving up, I'm sure of it. Do you think it might be some kind of sign, you know, him being there? I mean, the way he looked at me, it sent shivers down my spine, almost as though he knew me, knew everything about me, as if he knows what's coming?'

Susan consoled him, leaning forward in her chair, her hands drawing warmth from her own hot mug.
'Ronnie, look there obviously is someone lurking about in the garden but it's not a spirit or a ghost it's just a man! I wonder if we should get the police involved. After all, if he's on private property and he's not a customer, then he should leave.'

She put down her mug on the cork mat on the side table and got up to hug Ronnie close.

'We'll go and see the Doctor again, shall we, tomorrow, let's see if you can be referred to a specialist or a consultant, or someone? We mustn't give up Ronnie, you will be well again, you'll see and no more smoking ok? Starting from today; it's important Ronnie, you must quit.'

Ronnie looked down at her upturned face, her liquid blue eyes holding on to unshed tears and resignedly he nodded his agreement. He reached inside his trouser pocket and felt the crumpled cigarette packet there. He pulled it out slowly and held it in his hand. There were three left in the box. As he took his last long look it was almost as though he was saying goodbye to an old friend and then quickly, before he had time to change his mind, he threw it unceremoniously into the bin.

Dr Meadows, the respiratory specialist, sent Ronnie for some blood tests, x-rays and a scan. About two months later, they were called back to Dr Meadows' office. He gave Ronnie the grave news that he had developed an invasive fungus called Aspergillus which had in fact been growing on his lungs for quite some time. Although the news was not good and everyone knew it, there was almost a silent accord that no one would speak about any prognosis Ronnie might have.

Ronnie was given the disappointing news by the specialist that he must stop working at the restaurant immediately as the fumes and the heat in the kitchen atmosphere were not helping his condition and so from then on it was Dougie who had to take the strain and who was effectively in charge. Jean and Susan obviously helped as much as they could and Nana Win and Grandad George pitched in too and so they were able to carry on with the business.

Strangely, Dougie quickly began to realise just how much he had come to rely on Ronnie, not so much for the physical chores, but definitely for his help and guidance; just to be able to discuss issues around staffing or food or even the lousy landlord. He had been able to bounce things off Ronnie and they would have a laugh together about any problems so that suddenly they became less of a burden. A problem shared is a problem halved he supposed. Ronnie was the older brother and Dougie had always looked up to him and idolised him but he was also very protective of him, undoubtedly due to his illness, and there had never been any competition between them like other brothers. They loved and respected each other and always pulled together and so Dougie would miss him not being around every day.

Ronnie was given strict instructions about a regime of physiotherapy and medication. If he stuck to the course of treatment then he could be hopeful about seeing some improvement in his lungs. He was to breathe in an antifungal pesticide, via a face mask, and Fiona became used to seeing the frighteningly large gas type cylinders lined up along the wall in her Uncle's bedroom when she visited the house. He would be semi-sitting, propped up against the dark wooden headboard by three or four soft white pillows and he would gaze at her sadly from behind a see-thru plastic mask covering his nose and mouth and which was held in place by elastic loops around both of his ears. Fiona hated to see him like that and could almost see the apology in his eyes. She felt sad for him and utterly helpless.

Susan had her role to play in his physiotherapy regime by having to routinely pummel Ronnie's back whilst he lay on his stomach, over the bed. The idea was to loosen any debris inside his lungs which he would then have to cough up to clear his chest. The debris was a hard and chalky substance making him retch and vomit whenever it got stuck in the back of his throat which was very often. After a few months Fiona sadly realised that she could see no improvement in her Uncle. He was becoming thin and gaunt. She could see the signs, remembering Aunt Evelyn.

The ghostly sightings increased at the restaurant.

Katy, one of the waitresses, was very excited one morning telling everyone that she had definitely seen a monk standing in the corner of the corridor the previous evening. She recounted the story to them all that she had returned to the restaurant after having left her coat on the coat rack just outside Anna's room. She had come in through the back door, glad to find it still open, but that Mr and Mrs Fordham were obviously upstairs in the big room probably watching telly as there was no one about downstairs and so she had quickly grabbed her coat and just as she had turned round to put it on, she had seen him, standing behind her, just outside the cellar door.

'He was there, standing right there behind me, he was, as large as life!' she said gabbling away with enthusiasm. 'He was a big feller and he just stood there in the corner. He had on a dark cloak with a big hood over his face so I couldn't see his features at all, it was a bit murky there in the corner and he seemed to merge into the shadows a bit, but I did see that he had a thick belt round his middle, more like a rope than a belt, but it was tied right round him it was and hanging down at the front of him, just like Friar Tuck!'

After than she said she couldn't quite remember what happened but she thought she must have screamed and then she ran as fast as she could, back the way she had come, through Anna's room and then out through the back door and home.

Fiona listened to these stories with alarm while others laughed and scoffed at them with derision. They worried her but she had promised to say nothing to anyone about Alf or the tunnel. She didn't want to get involved in it any more. Now that she was home, safe and sound, she silently swore to herself that she would never venture anywhere near the tunnel again? She knew Alf had more secrets which he did not want to share with her, like the clandestine recovery of the sword, and what that was all about? It did intrigue her though and she still could not get him or their weird and wonderful adventure out of her mind.

One day when the restaurant was very quiet with only two customers in Anna's room the Fordham family had taken themselves upstairs to watch a race and Fiona was wandering around aimlessly and suddenly she thought she would seek him out. She wondered whether he knew anything about the strange sightings and why they were becoming more frequent. On this occasion he was easy to find as he was out in the courtyard garden, digging and planting. It was a beautiful hot sunny day and she sat down nearby on the green garden seat under the lilac tree watching him while he worked. Alf did not look round but he knew she was there; he could feel her eyes upon him.

He had tried to avoid her as much as possible since their journey through the tunnel but the secret they shared was so potent he hadn't been able to get her out of his mind but he knew he must keep away. She was trouble whichever way he looked at it and there was still important work to be done now that he had recovered the sword.

'Hi Alf' she greeted him light-heartedly hoping he would stop and turn around to look at her but he just kept on digging. His shirt looked too big for him and it was shabby and torn.

She persevered, 'I haven't seen you for a while. Is everything OK?'

Alf stopped digging and turned to look at her. He could sense her curiosity and was determined to be guarded.

'Yes', he said cautiously, 'everything is fine, how are things in Marshalswick?' he asked politely.

She stared at his face probing for any hint of tenderness or genuine interest but he turned back to his digging denying her any further exploration of his features.

She sighed, 'It's ok I suppose, a little bit boring and predictable but its a nice suburban housing estate with a few shops at the quadrant and wheat fields nearby for country walks and of course it's not far from town,' she answered smiling, 'it's only about half an hour's walk if you wanted to come and visit?'

He gave no answer and continued with his digging.

She paused for a while, enjoying the sound of his spade as it turned over the earth, listening to his heavy breathing from the physical exertion.

'I haven't forgotten our little adventure', she prompted expectantly.

Again he said nothing and continued with his task of preparing a bed ready for planting nasturtiums.

She watched his muscles rippling beneath his thin shirt. His brown wavy hair had grown longer and hung down swinging backwards and forwards in time with the shifting motion of the spade.

'What did you do with the sword?' she asked 'Have you still got it?'

After a few seconds he stopped what he was doing and turned to face her. Slowly he lowered himself onto his haunches so that his warm face was level with hers. He wiped the shining sweat from his forehead with the back of his sleeve and then tucking his damp hair behind his ear he spoke to her in soft sombre tones.

'Fiona, please,' he almost begged, clutching his spade like a prop as he fell silent. She waited quietly, with her hands tucked under her knees, wanting him to say more, enjoying this intimacy.

'Look, I understand you want to know more about what happened. You're young and inquisitive and it's to be expected. But there are many mysteries in this world and you will learn, as you get older, not to meddle with things which are out of your control. All that I told you is my problem, mine alone, do you hear? I sincerely thank you for keeping my secret. But I strongly suggest that you now get on with your life and try not to think about it.'

As he spoke the words aloud, he knew it was hopeless. She was like a limpet clinging to a rock and he knew he was the rock. He stood up and removed his neck scarf wiping his brow with it. She watched as a bead of sweat trickled down his neck, pooling in the hollow just above his collar bone. She couldn't take her eyes off it and swallowed hard as a powerful urge to lean forward and taste it threatened to overcome her. She tried to block the image from her mind and cleared her throat quickly as she whispered.

'I….I just wanted to ask you something about the tunnel,' she said, hesitant to say more, as his piercing gaze once again rested on her flushed cheeks.

'Is there a chance, or rather is it possible that a person who enters the tunnel could maybe have come from a different time, I mean, not necessarily from your time?' she queried, ignoring his earlier warning.

Alf sighed and bowed his head again. After a short pause he looked up.

'Try not to think about it will you? There is a lot about the tunnel that still confounds me even after all my years of going down there and searching for a way back. It seems there are many side passages and exits which can suddenly appear and disappear. I have not dared to try any of them for fear of where they might lead and that is why I am warning you to stay away from it. Do you hear me?'

She distracted herself by looking at the holes he had just been digging, and she watched as a small smooth worm probed and wriggled its way out into the sunlight.

While she became slightly mesmerised by the small creature he leaned nearer to her, his closeness causing her to catch her breath. Silently he lifted her chin gently with the knuckle of his forefinger and found himself gazing into the depths of gentle violet eyes. He couldn't help himself as he looked down at her soft young mouth and the urge to kiss those yielding open lips was almost beyond his control. They both knew they shared a secret so profound it joined them together, linking them forever. Fiona felt the bond between them growing and she knew he felt it too. He knew more about the secret of the tunnel than he was divulging she felt sure of it.

She felt safe with him though and she wanted him to hold her again as he'd held her in that fantasy world of theirs. She flushed at the pattern of her thoughts and felt as if a fever had suddenly taken hold of her;

'Who is the cavalier?' she gasped hastily, rushing on to cover her discomfort, 'do you think he has come through the tunnel as well?'

Obviously her probing had gone too far as Alf pulled away from her abruptly and stood up starting to pick up his tools. He must get away now. She was asking too many questions, drawing him in, and he recognised he was finding it harder and harder to resist her. He must stay away from her at all costs.

Chapter Twenty Six:

Anna stood at the doorway to the garden after her last two customers had gone. She had decided to take a break and breathe in some of the fresh spring air when she saw Fiona sitting on the wrought iron seat. The seat had been painted green a few years before, but now it had become rather rusty and the paint was flaking badly.   Anna walked over to the chair and sat down gingerly next to her 'little angel' as she used to call her.

'What's the matter Liebelein? Let me share your troubles!'

Fiona looked up and forced a smile, rousing from her reverie. However much she wanted to share her story, no one would ever believe her, and so she must stay silent.

'Hello Anna, I'm fine, I was just lost in thought that's all! I hear it's been a bit quiet in there today.'

'Yes it has and I just don't know why' Anna sighed, 'the weather is so beautiful today; you would think people would be out and about, doing things together.'

'Yes, I suppose so, but then again maybe being outside in the sunshine is more appealing than sitting inside a stuffy restaurant. It's getting warmer now; perhaps they're all down at the lake having a picnic.'

'Hmm may be you are right Liebchen but I do know your Father and Grandfather are very worried about the numbers. I heard them talking about it earlier, and it is making them all so anxious especially your father, but we will be busy again, I'm sure' she exclaimed positively.

'Anna, you're so right, what you are saying is true! I see everyone worrying about the restaurant and the future. The customers seem to be dwindling, Uncle Ronnie is not well, and Nana and Grandad aren't getting any younger, how much longer can we keep going? I feel something is going to have to change.'

'Don't you worry your young head about that' replied Anna in a motherly tone, 'I am certain people will be eating here for many years to come, not only because of the low prices but for the quality and quantity of food on their plates. There is nowhere else in town offering such generous portions, why would they want to go anywhere else?'

Fiona smiled, 'Yes, well I'd like to agree with you Anna but there are many other restaurants opening up and down the town and the difference is they're all serving alcohol and that seems to be what people want now; they enjoy having a glass of wine with their meal, it's definitely becoming more popular now.'

'Hmm, well, we'll see, I think maybe we have a few years left. People are fickle, and fashions come and go but they always like a bargain and that's definitely what they get here, a starter, a good hot meal and a dessert all for just £3, now where else can they get that?'

'Well, I hope you're right Anna. I really do.'

They sat contentedly for a while in companionable silence.

'By the way how is poor old Fred getting on?' Fiona asked, remembering that things had not been going so well for Anna and her husband recently.

She remembered with dismay that that Anna's husband Fred had been a constant source of amusement for the children many years before when she and her cousins had been younger and sillier.

He was a good kind man who arrived at the restaurant on a Saturday afternoon to collect Anna after her busy day at work and he would stand waiting for her at his favourite place next to the drinks cabinet, holding his smart trilby hat in his hand, chatting away to the children in his amiable way. His bald head would continuously bounce and nod uncontrollably just like the nodding dogs on the back shelf of a car. The children would snigger and laugh behind his back at this strange shaking mannerism and Fiona had only learned a lot later about the dreadful affliction of Parkinson's disease and she'd felt terribly guilty about her past mistreatment of Fred.   Anna and Fred were such a lovely couple. They never seemed bitter about what life had thrown at them, always looking on the bright side and even though they had never been lucky enough to have children of their own both of them considered the children of The Pilgrims Rest as nearest to their own.

'Oh he's not too bad, thank you my little spätchen,' Anna replied.   'His shaking is still awful but that's nothing new and there's nothing that seems to help with that anyway. We've tried everything! His memory is getting worse now as well, sometimes he looks at visitors who come to the house and I can tell he doesn't know who they are. He's not sleeping very well at night either so he's decided to move himself out of our bedroom and into the spare room which is all very sad after 45 years of marriage, isn't it my lieibchen? But at least he is getting more sleep, and for that matter so am I!' she said laughing at full volume, 'yes, yes', she sighed, 'it's a lot better now we are getting more sleep and we are not so 'murrisch' - ha ha that is the German word for being bad-tempered - and so thankfully we are coping quite well at the moment.'

Anna gave Fiona a brief tight hug and kissed the top of her head hurriedly,

'Well I suppose I'd better clear away the tables', Anna said standing up and smoothing down her apron, 'you can help me if you like? Luckily some tables are already laid ready for tomorrow which will save me quite a bit of time.'

'Oh yes, yes, of course I will' Fiona agreed readily 'I'll go and get a tray, won't be a minute'

She left her seat and exited the sunshine of the pretty courtyard garden by heading under the small archway at the back of the garden and into the damp darkness of the outbuildings behind the scullery.

As her eyes adjusted from the bright daylight she saw her father standing just inside the doorway at his usual place, leaning against the door handle, with a half burned cigarette in his brown and yellow stained fingers. He gave her an indulgent smile.

'Dad', she sighed, 'I thought you were going to give up that habit since Uncle Ronnie has been so ill. What do you think you're doing?' she scolded him.

He chuckled; using his favourite defence mechanism of laughter, always worthwhile to diffuse any awkward situation; 'don't you worry about me' he said smugly 'I'm one of the lucky ones.'

She gave up on her self-righteousness. She wasn't in the mood to lecture him today. Well, I'm going to help Anna clear the tables, aren't I good' she said and then cheekily ventured 'any chance of some extra wages for helping Anna with that?'

Still smiling Dougie ploughed his hand deep into his trouser pocket bringing back out a large wad of notes. He licked his thumb and generously peeled off a tenner.

'There you go, good girl, now go and earn it!'

When Ronnie was admitted to hospital, everyone tried their best to be optimistic. Jean and Dougie went with Susan to visit him at the Royal London. On that day he was going to have an exploratory surgical procedure and they'd gone to wish him luck. A radioactive dye called a tracer was to be injected into a vein in his groin. This would then travel through his body to collect in the lung area and x-ray imaging would allow them to see what was going on.

Jean realised immediately she saw him in the hospital bed that Ronnie did not look at all well. She saw that his skin was grey and clammy as she leaned in to kiss his forehead and to whisper good wishes for his speedy recovery. As she backed away from his bed, he looked up at her one more time, and she witnessed the tangible fear and foreboding in his eyes. The sheer terror on his face that day would remain in her memory forever.

Less than a week later he had passed away.

Fiona felt bad as she had sent him a 'joke' get well card to the hospital and she hoped and prayed he hadn't read it before he died although maybe it might have cheered him up in his hour of need. It had been a funny card with a man in a hospital bed completely bandaged from head to foot but she would never have sent it if she had known how close to death he was. Her tears welled at the thought.

Sadder still was the effect the devastating news had on her father. He was inconsolable and remained in utter disbelief for many hours after the news came through.

It seemed to Fiona that a part of Dougie had died as well. He'd hugged her hard, embarrassingly hard, like he'd never hugged her before, as though he was trying to draw some kind of solace from his first born. She was the balm for his open wound. Fiona had tried to hug him back in the same way but she didn't really know how. It didn't feel right somehow, to see that side of him. He'd always been the joker, the one who laughed until he cried and who always saw the funny side of things. Fiona just didn't know how to be this sad person with him. It was new territory and she didn't like it at all. When Uncle Ronnie died he took with him the fun, the laughter, and the joy of life. It was also the first nail in the coffin for The Pilgrims Rest.

In order to fill the large gaping hole left by Ronnie's death, Dougie began to watch a psychic medium on the television. He was searching for answers to his own personal questions about life and death, seeking some sort of comfort as he thrashed around in the loneliness of his grief. He began to fervently believe in life after death and that the spirits of loved ones were still within our reach and that we could still communicate with them and this notion seemed to comfort him and made him happy.

He became convinced that everything the medium said was completely and utterly true and he would not listen to any opinion to the contrary. Dougie would lecture the family at every possible opportunity trying to convince everyone around him to believe as he did. He talked obsessively about 'the other side' remaining adamant that he wasn't a religious man and did not trust in God. His church was the television set and his belief, that death was not the end.

'We will all be reborn' he repeated many times, 'and all our illnesses and ailments will be gone and we will be perfect again.'

Probing jibes came from those who scorned his fanatical stance; 'How old will we be then?' the questions came.

'In the prime of life - thirty two' he'd answer wholeheartedly,

'But what happens if you die before you're thirty two?' the others jeered trying to trick him.

He'd smile then, knowingly, scathingly admonishing them for their doubt. His knowledge was prophetic and he would not let them deny it.

Eventually the family gave up allowing him to think what he liked because disagreeing with him was futile. In fact they started to humour him rather like a wayward child. He wasn't causing any harm to anyone and it gave him a reason and a purpose for life to carry on.

And life did continue, as it always had at The Pilgrims Rest, for a while at least. The world hadn't ended, not yet, not quite, although it felt like that for a while. But, bit by bit, little by little, the pieces were picked up and put back together again and the family continued, at least for a while.

Nana Win dampened down her emotions more than ever before. She shut herself off from the rest of the family and after lunchtime she would disappear upstairs as soon as the last customer had left, finding sanctuary in her big room where she would watch her big television slipping ever further into her protective shell. Outwardly she showed none of the grief she was feeling at the loss of her eldest son.

The restaurant continued to struggle and limped on for a while but as enthusiasm for the task gradually dwindled the remaining family members agreed that they should cut their losses and sell up while there was enough in the bank for them all to be able to retire and live fairly comfortably.

The staff members were given the news, and all those who had been loyal and steadfast throughout the years, were very understanding. Anna agreed it was about time she retired and admitted at last to everyone that she was 75!! Who would have believed it, the way she charged around with so much energy!

It was the end of an era but there were mixed feelings of sadness but also an immense feeling of relief and anticipation of what lay ahead, particularly for Jean who had absolutely no regrets and was glad it was now over and she looked forward to a new chapter in her life, hopefully going back to her old life and continuing her secretarial career. She was still young, only 50. She was excited!

Of course a big party was held to celebrate the occasion and as the last day drew to a close and all the customers had gone, staff and family congregated once more in Anna's Room, just like at Christmas, only this was different, this would be the last time. There would be no more Christmas gatherings.

Fiona lay awake at night during those last few weeks at the restaurant and thought about Alf? What would happen to him once they'd all left? She went to find her Nana Win. After all she was the one who had taken him in all those years ago. She had a responsibility to him. Where would he go?

Nana Win was sitting on her favourite chair in the big room staring at the TV screen in front of her.

'Nana what's going to happen to Alf', she asked almost accusingly.

'He wants to stay here' Win answered blankly.

'But how can he? We're selling up. The new owners won't let him stay will they?'

At last Win got up and reached forward to turn down the volume on the television set. She returned to her seat and briefly looked round at her granddaughter,

'Well, yes they will actually. They have said he can stay upstairs in his room for now and have asked that he keep an eye on the place until they move in and then if he wants to he can help them with all their removals and refurbishing the place, so that'll keep him occupied for a while.'

'What about the other lodgers?' Fiona asked, 'are they staying as well?'

'No, no, now look stop worrying dear, they are both leaving and they've found other places to live so in actual fact it'll only be Alf left here on his own for a short while. It appears the new owners don't want to move in to the building straight away, not until July apparently, so he'll be here on his own just for a few weeks.'

'Oh, I see,' Fiona considered this bit of information with alarm and thought there was no way she would ever want to remain in this spooky place on her own!

She finally voiced her fears;

'That'll be a bit strange for him, won't it, Nan. I mean he'll be completely alone in this huge empty place?'

'Yes, I know but it's his choice so I'm not asking him again.'

Nana Win returned to the television and turned up the volume once more indicating that in her opinion the conversation was over. Her attention span was extremely short these days, probably a deliberate tactic to avoid any further probing questions, and Fiona quickly realised she'd been dismissed.

The next few weeks at the restaurant were extremely busy. The dining furniture from each of the rooms, tables, chairs, even paintings on the walls were all sold off or given to family or friends if they were interested and all of the kitchen equipment was cleared out and sold off very cheaply. The new owners were not interested in any of it as they were a furniture retailer and so they wanted every room completely gutted.

Fiona was devastated when she heard the news that the exotic dining furniture which she cherished as a fundamental part of her heritage and which had adorned and romanticised the big room for as long as she could remember, had been sold without any consultation.

Apparently a tall gentleman in a dark suit had arrived from the London Auctioneers' Savills, to view the unusual set of furniture and he'd been asked to give a possible auction value.

Nana had recounted her story about its origin and that it had been shipped over from Indonesia during the nineteen fifties when the profits at the restaurant were buoyant and although she couldn't quite remember the total sum paid it was definitely a good few thousand. At that time Win and George could afford to buy the rather ostentatious dining set needed to fill the huge dimensions of the room.

The willowy gent was supercilious and showed disinterest at first but finally in a somewhat patronizing manner he offered the paltry sum of five hundred pounds with a 'generous' free collection thrown in as if he was doing them a favour. With a sigh and wanting to be shot of the whole caboodle, Win agreed and signed on the dotted line.

Fiona was mortified when she'd found out and once more went to see Win to see if anything could be done to call a halt to it.

'But Nana, surely someone in the family could have kept it!' she lamented.

'It was too big' Win defended herself loudly, 'I couldn't take it with me to the new flat and none of your houses had enough room, so it had to go!'

Fiona studied her Nan's blank unyielding expression, feeling helpless.   There it was again, a complete lack of sentimentality and emotion.   Didn't she care? May be she couldn't care, wouldn't allow herself to care.   There was nothing Fiona could do to change her Nana Win's resolute stance, her grandmother was devoid of all feeling she was sure of it and she would leave the Pilgrims Rest, her home of over twenty years, without a second look.

But what Fiona didn't realise was that Win did care. She cared more than anyone would ever know. The pain inside her chest was like a lead weight threatening to suffocate her as it dragged her downwards, drowning her in the depths of her own misery. The pain of losing Ronnie was unimaginable, so much worse than losing her baby girl all those years ago, she didn't get a chance to know the baby, she was a stranger, but Ronnie was known and loved, he was her first born, he was special. She'd always felt guilty about his illness and wondered whether she could have done something to prevent it from happening. The only way she could cope with the anguish she felt was to switch it off inside her head just like the switch on the television which she could switch on and immerse herself in whatever was on; horse race, comedy show, soap opera, it didn't matter what it was as long as she could forget the ache in her heart, even just for a short while, and her hope was that in time the pain would diminish.

Chapter Twenty Seven:

Once The Pilgrims Rest had been cleared of its many years of accumulated belongings, it looked dirty, dingy and derelict. Without occupants the life and soul of the place had been stripped away.

Win and George had managed to purchase a small flat in Marshalswick which was in the Ridgeway just around the corner from Jean and Dougie and they were really looking forward to moving in to it. It seemed Dougie would be busy with his new career as carer looking after the needs of his elderly parents and ferrying them about as their taxi driver and chauffeur.

When all the final goodbyes had been warmly given to staff and customers alike Win and George moved out of their home of over twenty years and in to the ground floor flat in Marshalswick. They had taken with them a few carefully chosen pieces of furniture from the big room and Jean had arranged for new carpets and curtains to be fitted to give the place a homely feel.

George still enjoyed the comfort of his favourite wing back armchair with the clawed feet and sat in it throne-like surveying his rather diminished kingdom. Unfortunately his dynamic personality seemed to shrink significantly as well as he sat quietly in the corner of the room, a silent observer for much of the time. His new hearing aid had been discarded as a nuisance contraption and he became more and more isolated from any conversations that took place. When the family visited he would pipe up half way through a conversation to talk about something completely arbitrary and off kilter with the rest of the discussion and in her consistently merciless fashion, Win would shout at him;

'Oh, shut up George, we're not talking about that any more we're talking about something else now!'

George would slump back into his armchair again retreating once more into his own quiet world, his bottom lip thrust out like a petulant child.

Occasionally Fiona would find a stool and sit next to him companionably wanting to talk to him on her own, just the two of them, in the corner of the room away from all the other chitchat and this was a much better arrangement for him. He would enjoy telling her interesting facts about the past, about how a pint used to cost a penny and how you could live on a loaf of bread for a whole week at the cost of a mere ha'penny. He always took great pleasure in passing on his wise words to her, like his secret for a long life, which was to have a 'whisky chaser' every evening about an hour or so after dinner. When he saw her mystified look, he elaborated that this was a pint of beer, followed shortly afterwards by a small glass of whisky. He would chuckle huskily at her look of surprise and Fiona would then watch the movement of his chest, as it shook up and down, his face turning bright red at the effort of it all.

Back at the restaurant, Alf was down in the cellar.

The relief he felt at being alone was tangible. At last they had all gone and he could concentrate on the important role he was about to play.

He had returned the sword to its rightful place during a late night visit to the Abbey and now it lay safe in its hiding place once more inside the marble base at the Shrine of Saint Alban. He hoped and prayed it would remain there untouched for many years to come. The precious map he had retrieved from the sword was carefully folded inside his back pocket and the key contained within his bible had been removed and was now swinging on a long cord tied around his neck.

He entered the tunnel once more and at intervals he retrieved the map to study it as he tried to follow the hazy trail marked. He moved forwards slowly searching with his hands as he explored its cavernous reaches. It must be here somewhere, a keyhole for the key?

He thanked the Lord that he had been given this precious time, with no interruptions, no disturbances, no chattering customers, and more importantly no inquisitive family members to worry about. He felt sure that some kind of divine providence had intervened and allowed him this opportunity to discover the mystery of the tunnel and its secret treasure but he had to find this out soon or the valuable time he'd been given would run out.

He thought back nearly 18 years to his first journey through the tunnel.

In his precious bible he had secreted an ancient key which had been given to him by William the Monk, his mentor and friend. The key was about three inches long and made of bronze with the shape of three crosses on its flank and 7 holes in its circular head. It was fairly heavy and bulky, not like modern keys.   William also told Alf about the secret prehistoric map hidden within the pommel of the roman gladius, the sword used to behead Saint Alban.   William warned him to keep the map and the key safe as they were sacred artefacts passed through the centuries from the first monastery founded here in the year 793 AD by King Offa of Mercia.

On that fateful day when Henry's soldiers had thundered into town invading the monastery and thrashing the monastic community with their swords and bludgeons Alf had taken William's advice and ran directly for the safety of the tunnel. A few moments after he had entered it the quietness surrounding him seemed to cushion his wounded soul and he began to feel a little safer and that was when he suddenly remembered the words of the Monk.

He had cursed himself for his haste. The bible with the key inside was safe in his hand following the morning gathering of Lauds, the daily praising of the return of light to earth and the eternal light from Christ. But he'd run thoughtlessly when he'd first heard the screaming and commotion outside, clutching the bible to him like a talisman, as he'd dashed through the tunnel. Sadly there had been no time to recover the sword which he had hidden in the orchard.

But that was in the past, for now here in his possession, he had both.

He was not certain what he might be searching for but after studying the map for some time it appeared to show various interlinking passageways leading downwards. He felt sure, if his bearings were correct, that he was still positioned underneath Holywell Hill but all was quiet above him. He had never ventured as far as this into the tunnel and certainly never in this direction before because previously his only intention had been to reach the Abbey. He was now well within the confines of the tunnel and appeared to have reached a dead end. He began to fear he was lost. The map was indistinct and faded but he could just make out an etching in the margin to the side of the trail which appeared to show a man with a staff in his hand pointing to a lighted area and what looked like a tomb within it but as he continued to search groping the ground and the wall still he could find nothing for the key to unlock.

As Alf started to lose faith he spoke aloud into the darkness which covered him;
'Oh Lord, help me please, what should I do here, what is it I must find?'

He knew how important it was for him to find an answer, a revelation, some kind of ultimate salvation to give meaning to all those years of solitude. He'd been so lonely. It seemed there was nowhere, no time nor place, where he could stay and belong, where he could lead a normal life. Was there another choice for him; an alternative to the barren existence he'd endured? The answer must surely lie here within the tunnel. His palms became sweaty and his heart started beating faster and faster. He could hardly breathe as he began to feel stifled from the lack of oxygen down here in the bowels of the earth and he began to feel drained of all energy and sick with fever.

A cold mist surrounded him and his breath formed in the air like droplets of heat frozen in the stillness. He tried to breathe but the icy air forced him to cover his face with the collar of his old trench coat as he peered through gritty eyes into the darkness.

A shuffling sound behind him made turn around so swiftly that he almost lost his balance. As he leant against the damp cold wall for support he slowly slid down the rough surface to the ground and peered ahead into the gloom. A misty glow seeped up from the ground and began to swirl and float in front of him, its fingers licking the walls and stroking the floor of the cavern as if it was a living breathing entity, and then he saw right in the middle of its eerie light a familiar figure standing in front of him; it was the cavalier.

Alf froze, staring in bewilderment at the vision before him.

Lifting his capotain hat from his head the cavalier gave a grand sweeping bow;

'Good morrow Brother Alf', he said benevolently.

Alf continued staring at him in confusion and dread as he recollected one other time when he had witnessed a vision of the Cavalier in the tunnel but not at such close proximity. At that time he thought it had merely been an apparition or illusion of some kind. It was during one of his many failed attempts to get back to his own time through the tunnel. He remembered he'd given up on his endeavour and was trying to return again back into the cellar through the opening but the gap in the wall could not be found.

Fear had begun to rise up that he had been trapped inside the tunnel with no escape. He'd looked around in panic and in the distance he had seen the cavalier walking slowly towards him. In abject horror he'd desperately tried one last time to get back into the cellar and this time luckily his hand had touched the smooth bricks around the hidden aperture and he had managed to haul himself back into the cellar before the wall finally closed behind him and he was safe inside the cellar.

The cavalier replaced his feathered hat with a flourish and stood with his hands on his hips, quiet and motionless, as he waited for Alf to recover himself.

Who are you?' enquired Alf, feeling extremely vulnerable and fearful of what might occur, 'why are you here?'

The cavalier smiled as he responded in a convivial manner oozing with charm and civility,

'Do not worry Alf! Please have no fear for I will do you no harm. My name is Robert, loyal defender of the catholic faith and the guardian of this tunnel and of its influence and power. It is indeed an honour to meet you here at this special place after all this time. You have done exceedingly well my dear friend. For many years, you have managed to keep the secret of the tunnel hidden away from prying eyes and I humbly thank you for your diligence.'

Alf still cowered slightly as he continued to study the cavalier. His trust in the man before him was still tentative and his confidence could not be gained at so short an acquaintance.

Robert was indeed a fine looking individual. His beard was full and fiery red, his hair was long and thick under his high pilgrim hat. His doublet of brown and gold brocade was of an intricate Spanish design, full of swirls and flourishes, with a double row of gold silk covered buttons proceeding very high at the neck and continuing down to a frilled V shape at the bottom. Each button was laced together with dark brown cord in a crisscross fashion at the front. A wide frilled collar of the purest white sat neatly on his shoulders and covering his thighs were full breeches of a slightly darker colour but with the same intricate Spanish design. A short black cloak was pushed back over his shoulder which hung down to his hip.

Alf recalled the various descriptions from other members of staff where sightings of the cavalier had been claimed but their images had always been vague and shadowy. He had never understood the connection between the cavalier and the tunnel but always worried and suspected that the cavalier was a ghostly harbinger of doom always appearing just before or after a moment of disaster or tragedy.

As he began to marvel at the cavalier a feeling of calmness and serenity started to soak into his very being. As he continued to bathe in its influence his fear and foreboding diminished and was at last replaced with admiration and awe for the man standing in front of him. Indeed as Robert welcomed him and beckoned him forwards in kindness and friendship Alf began to consider that the cavalier had been trying to protect them and perhaps only wanted to warn them about these calamitous events? In that moment a sudden epiphany embraced him that the purpose and meaning of his life was about to be revealed.

'I have the key' Alf said, confirming something he felt sure the cavalier already knew. Robert smiled encouragingly holding out his grey gloved hand,

'Come with me Alf,' he said, helping Alf up from his haunches so that he could stand albeit a little wobbly. The cavalier was a good head and shoulders taller than Alf, and he looked down at Alf's confused expression benevolently as he guided him carefully onwards towards a white light which shone ahead of them like a hovering orb lighting the tunnel as they walked.

A warm feeling of worship and dedication overcame Alf as he moved towards the light but as he grew closer a deeper feeling crept inside his soul, one he'd forgotten from a long time ago - love. He suddenly saw ahead of him an ornate wooden casket, densely decorated with knife cut narrative scenes. It appeared to be made of oak and there was an ancient lock fitted at the front. He saw the imagery was Christian, with depictions of the Adoration of the Magi, the Last Supper and further inscriptions written in Latin. The lid was adorned with a large ivory cross and it stood abutted against the tunnel wall raised on top of a white alabaster plinth. He realised why he had never seen it before as he'd never entered this section of the tunnel and without the map he probably would never have known it was here.

The cavalier manoeuvred Alf carefully towards the lock.

'You must use the key' he instructed Alf kindly.

Alf felt unsure and held the key close to his chest, his heartbeat was loud with trepidation, but when he saw only gentleness in the eyes of his new ally he bent his head forward slipping the cord from around his neck. Once he'd retrieved the heavy bronze key he carefully steered it towards the lock at the side of the casket. His hands trembled but the key was a perfect fit and slotted in to position easily. He looked up once more at Robert who was smiling down at him and nodding encouragingly as Alf turned the key gently in the lock and then they stood back away from it side by side and watched the lid of the casket slowly open.

A strange, unearthly sound was heard coming from inside the tomblike coffin and Alf backed away as a golden glow rose up from inside the coffin entering the atmosphere. He watched it creep along the walls of the tunnel, and heard a multitude of sighs as it increased in length and lustre. As he listened he discerned that they were not sighs of sadness but sighs of joy being emitted from the tunnel walls all around him. The light moved at speed seeming to fill the catacombs until a honeycomb of light shone all around him. He watched, entranced, and became joyful as it was now clear to him what was happening; the golden light from the tomb was gathering up all the lost souls, the souls of those trapped within the tunnel perhaps for many centuries, it was drawing them out of the walls and up into the light.

He saw that behind the cavalier an aperture was forming and becoming more and more visible in the tunnel wall. It was not like other passages within the tunnel. It was completely circular and the walls were smooth, not like rock but like a huge wormhole. The golden light travelled upwards and onwards towards the new opening in the wall behind the cavalier, lighting the area and showing the way.

'What is this?' asked Alf. 'Where does it lead?'

Robert moved towards Alf once more and holding out his gloved hand he drew Alf forward towards the intensifying light within the tunnel wall.

'Have no fear Alf, for this is all perfectly right and good. It is how it should be. You and you alone have released the spirit of Albanus and allowed his goodness and mercy to recover these abandoned souls now no longer trapped in the darkness, and now Brother Alfred, come, for it is now your time; time for you to find peace and harmony and an end to your long lonely journey. You will be rewarded for your devotion and steadfastness and your reward will be everlasting life.'

Alf looked beyond the cavalier in wonder and into the bright light emanating from the tunnel behind him. He could see a group of people, standing there in the light, and behind them more coming forwards, jostling, until a throng of people were standing there waiting to greet him. As his eyes became accustomed to the brightness he saw a child, a young girl standing shyly at the front of the small crowd, her hair was golden and her eyes, happy and radiant, rested upon him as she walked forward and reached up to him.

His jubilation and joy was unimaginable as he reached out once again to his beloved sister lost to him so long ago and now welcoming him into her arms.

THE END

EPILOGUE:

When they arrived home Jean seemed to have forgotten all about the note given to Fiona by the shop manager and she headed straight to the kitchen to prepare dinner.

'Do you want a cup of tea?' she called to Fiona who was already half way up the stairs.

'No thanks mum' Fiona called down 'I'm just going to my room for a while. I'll come and give you a hand later.'

'Ok dear, but don't worry, I can manage', her mother replied contentedly.

Fiona shut the door of her bedroom behind her and sat quietly on the edge of her bed. All was peaceful in the house apart from the distant sounds from the kitchen. Her siblings had gradually moved out one by one until she was now the only one left to keep her widowed mother company.

Sadly, the older members from the Fordham family firm had now passed away, firstly George, secondly Win and then third and not long after the others, Dougie, his elusive system on the horses remaining a distant dream never to materialise. He died quite suddenly in the end, his death caused by chronic obstructive pulmonary disease due to excessive smoke inhalation. Her own dear father gone, if only he'd heeded the warnings, she thought to herself, he would still be here now.

She looked down at the scrawled handwriting for a moment or two recalling those last few days at the restaurant nearly seven years ago.

She had returned to the restaurant a few months after it had closed, knowing the new owners had permanently moved in, and just wanting to find out if Alf was OK.

She had been told he'd gone away and although she'd tried to find out what had happened to him no one seemed to know. No one seemed interested either. It was as though he'd vanished as abruptly as he'd arrived and everyone just assumed he'd moved on to another town. She looked down at the envelope with misty eyes and carefully manoeuvred her finger under the flap easing it open. The slip of paper inside showed just one side of handwriting.

'My dearest Fiona,

What an adventure you and I had together, a sharing of heart and mind that would have fulfilled us both, and I am so full of sorrow that it had to end the way it did. You cannot imagine how many more secrets the tunnel has to tell. I know now there are many exits to different times and places, some wondrous, some terrifying, and so please do not venture down there again my dear. You asked me about the cavalier and I can assure you there is nothing to be afraid of. His name is Robert, a recusant and protector of the faith, and he remains the kindly guardian of the tunnel and its powers. I wish you and I could have been together in this life my beautiful Fiona but I know for certain we will meet again in another.

Godspeed

Alf

Printed in Poland
by Amazon Fulfillment
Poland Sp. z o.o., Wrocław